TASTES LIKE MURDER

AN ITALIAN-AMERICAN COZY MYSTERY SERIES
BOOK 3

M.P. BLACK

For my family—always with me wherever you are.

1

Early Monday morning, Angelica and I unlocked the front door to Moroni's Italian Bakery and Angelica stepped inside. She froze. She let out a sound, like the last air escaping a flat tire, and put a hand to her mouth.

"What?"

I stepped around her to see. Menus lay scattered across the cafe, chairs knocked over, the collection box for Mamma Mia's Helping Hand on the floor, split open, the donations gone. I moved toward the cash register. It, too, stood open and empty.

"What have they done?" Angelica said, clearly in shock.

"They've stolen all the cash," I said.

"The kitchen..."

"Wait."

I stopped her from crossing the café and going through the door in the back to the bakery. In my former career as an actress, I had starred in *Silver & Gold*, America's most popular detective show, and the experience had taught me a thing or two about crime.

In one episode, Eve Silver, my character, and her partner, Adam Gold, had investigated an apparent burglary, only to find an assassin waiting inside. A crime boss had hired him to take revenge on the detectives. It was an implausible plot. But it still made me cautious.

"Let's call the police," I suggested. "They can take a look."

We stepped into the street, where I called Chief Tedesco on my phone. She promised to be there in two minutes.

While Angelica and I waited, I put an arm around her shoulders. She was trembling.

"I can't believe it..." she said.

She stared, glassy eyed, at the front door.

The bakery was her baby, the source of her unshakeable optimism. To me, it was a safe haven.

Shortly after I'd come to Carmine, New Jersey, as part of the witness protection program (I had testified against my co-star in *Silver & Gold* in his drug- and arms-trafficking trial), I'd been accused of murder. Angelica gave me a job at the bakery. Moroni's sweetened everyone's life in Carmine. For me, it had also acted as a charm against all the bad luck.

Though no longer in witness protection, I still relied on Moroni's for a sense of normality.

I glanced at Angelica. For her, Moroni's was everything.

"I can't believe it..." she repeated.

I gave her shoulder a little squeeze.

Soon, a police cruiser, with its lights flashing, turned onto Garibaldi Avenue. It was still too early for Carmine's main street to come alive, and the other stores, shuddered and shadowy, wouldn't open for another couple of hours.

The cruiser pulled up to the curb.

Chief Tedesco stepped out of the car. She walked with her shoulders first, like an ice-hockey player, and in her well-fitted, dark-blue uniform, her body looked padded. Her keen eyes zeroed in on Angelica, me, and then the front door as she strode toward us.

I let out a sigh of relief. I was glad she'd arrived. We had started out enemies, but now we were friends, and her presence put me at ease.

"What happened?" she asked.

"Burglary."

"Did you see any perps?"

I shook my head. "But we didn't look in the back, just in case."

"Smart."

The driver stepped out of the police cruiser. Officer Anthony Ferrante. He proceeded more cautiously than his boss. Not because he was inexperienced or afraid of burglars, but because of me.

He smiled sheepishly as he approached and waved, then dropped his hand to his belt, as if he'd regretted the gesture.

"Bernie," he muttered.

"Hi, Anthony."

He scratched the back of his neck.

"You all right?"

He wasn't asking about the burglary. Anthony and I had dated until I'd discovered him cheating with another woman, and I'd ended it. Since then, he'd been as awkward as a schoolboy caught stealing. I was over him. Still, he'd done a rotten thing, and it didn't hurt for him to squirm a little.

"I'm fine," I said. "The bakery isn't."

"Come on, Ferrante," Chief Tedesco said, and Anthony looked relieved to be pulled away.

Angelica and I waited in the street as the two cops roamed the bakery to take stock of what had happened.

After a while, Chief Tedesco came out.

"We've checked the premises. The burglars are gone. Officer Ferrante is inspecting the damage. They broke through the back door. Looks like they used a crowbar. Unsophisticated work. But they weren't complete *chooches* because they'd disabled the security camera in the back alley. Hit it with a rock. But we may have some luck checking the security camera from Carlo's Restaurant next door."

"Why would anyone want to do such a thing?" Angelica asked.

I knew it wasn't a rhetorical question. Angelica could find goodness in the most wicked person, and while no one was more imaginative with Italian baked goods, she struggled to comprehend why one person would hurt another. Her world view might be unrealistic, but I loved her for it—one ounce of her kindness spread more joy than a thousand realists ever could, myself included.

"Most burglars take the easy way," Chief Tedesco said, skirting Angelica's question. "Grab what they can and get out quick. We constantly see this. I bet they took cash and laptops and anything else that's easy to sell."

"You see this all the time?" Angelica said, a look of horror on her face.

"All the time," Chief Tedesco confirmed.

"That's terrible."

Ah, that was my Angelica—immediately thinking of all the other poor victims of burglary. She engaged Chief Tedesco in a conversation about who'd gotten burgled recently, making sympathetic sounds at each anecdote.

As we were standing on the sidewalk, I noticed two people approaching us. A man and a woman, each wearing business suits. As they came closer, I recognized them: Mayor Tom Blink and Deputy Mayor Kathryn Palumbo.

"What's happened?" Deputy Mayor Palumbo said.

"Burglary," Chief Tedesco said.

"Crime is clearly increasing," Mayor Blink said. "You'll have to do something about that, Chief Tedesco."

"Mayor, burglaries have declined significantly over the past five years," Chief Tedesco said. "I report the numbers to you and everyone else on a monthly basis."

"Well, that's excellent news." The mayor grinned. "I knew my tough-on-crime initiative would pay off."

Before turning away, Chief Tedesco glanced at me and rolled her eyes, showing me what she thought of the mayor.

Mayor Blink turned to Angelica. "You'll be glad to get some joyful news this morning. The deputy mayor and I bring good tidings: The town council committee on the Italian Day Celebration has accepted your application."

Angelica blinked, clearly confused.

"For the contract to cater the event with Carlo," Deputy Mayor Palumbo explained, apparently trying to jog Angelica's memory.

Angelica's eyes widened. "You mean we got the job?"

Mayor Blink smiled. "You got the job."

Angelica turned to me, a smile on her face as well.

"Carlo put in the application—he'll handle savory food, and I'll handle baked goods and desserts. I can't believe we got the job."

"That is great news," I said.

"See, Bernie, even when things look dark, there is light."

I was genuinely glad to hear it. Angelica could use a pleasant distraction after the awfulness of the burglary.

My mind wasn't so easily distracted by good news, though.

As Angelica discussed logistics with the mayor and deputy mayor, I peered through the front window of Moroni's. I shielded my hands to get a clear view.

Anthony stood behind the counter. He opened a drawer, frowned at its contents, closed it again. He opened another drawer, frowned at its contents, closed it again. It seemed he wasn't finding any clues.

A couple of minutes later, Chief Tedesco emerged, with Anthony trailing behind.

"Angelica, I'd like to ask you some questions," she said. "You too, Bernie."

We stood in a cluster of pairs: Angelica and me, Chief Tedesco and Anthony, Mayor Blink and Deputy Mayor Palumbo. Chief Tedesco stared at the mayor and deputy mayor, a frown on her face.

Mayor Blink smiled. "Go ahead, don't mind us."

"Mayor, this is a police investigation."

"Oh, we won't get in your way."

"You're getting in the way right now," she said.

There was an awkward silence. Chief Tedesco staring at Mayor Blink made it more awkward. The mayor glanced at his shoes, over at Angelica and me, then at the sky. Finally, he turned his attention to his watch. "Well, I have a busy day ahead, anyway. No point in me hanging around a crime scene."

We watched the mayor and deputy mayor walk down Garibaldi Avenue. A couple of blocks down, Mayor Blink glanced over his shoulder, an anxious frown on his face.

"All right, Angelica and Bernie," Chief Tedesco said, all business again, "can you describe what you saw when you arrived this morning?"

Angelica explained the door had been locked and then described the mess we'd seen inside. She seemed less fazed by it all now, the good news about the town celebration coloring everything else.

"You came to work early," Chief Tedesco said, directing her question at me.

I nodded. "Because of the Johnny Greco murder, I've been behind on work. I wanted to make it up to Angelica."

Chief Tedesco nodded, understanding at once. She herself had congratulated me on my sleuthing, repeatedly thanking me for my help with solving the Greco case.

"There was cash in the register, Angelica. But you have a safe in your office. Why wasn't the cash put away?"

"I've never felt a need to. When the cash register fills up, I might put the cash in the register or even run it over to the bank, but honestly, Carmine is the safest place on Earth. Why would I worry?"

Chief Tedesco and I exchanged glances. Angelica's Carmine was rose-tinted, a lovely place to live, and somehow her vision of that world hadn't been tainted by the murder investigations I'd been involved with.

After a few more routine questions, Chief Tedesco asked us to follow her inside so Anthony could catalog what had been stolen.

I stepped inside Moroni's and the shock washed over me yet again. The café was such a mess, with chairs overturned and menus thrown across the floor. How could anyone be cruel enough to tear up this beautiful bakery? And who would steal from the collection box for Mamma Mia's, which supported single mothers in need? That was low.

But apart from the disorder, as Chief Tedesco had predicted, the burglars had done little harm: They'd grabbed cash and, as far as we could tell, nothing else.

The bakery out back was relatively untouched. A few metal bowls lay scattered on the floor, along with a handful of spatulas. But that was it. Angelica stepped into the small backroom office and pointed at her desk.

"See, things aren't so bad. They didn't even take my laptop." She opened the desk drawer. "And look, I left a pair of crystal earrings, and they missed those, too. How lucky!"

She held up a pair of glittering, teardrop earrings that would have tempted any magpie.

Angelica was right. She was lucky. Or else the burglars had been sloppy.

2

In the days that followed, Angelica got busy preparing for the Italian Day Celebration. She often stepped over to her brother's restaurant or Carlo came over to the bakery for coffee and a cookie. I was relieved to see Angelica get over the burglary so easily, though I found it harder to let go. Every morning, I arrived at work with a rock in the pit of my stomach, fully expecting to find that Moroni's had been broken into again.

Even during the busy workday, I couldn't shake the feeling that I'd missed an important detail about the burglary, but what was it?

Wednesday afternoon, as we closed the bakery for the day, my friend Nat Natale turned up.

Nat, with his blue eyes and floppy fair hair that was forever falling into his eyes, had been my first real friend in Carmine, and within no time, he'd become my bestie. When I'd been in witness protection, he, a big Eve Silver fan, had quickly worked out who I really was. But instead of revealing my true identity, he had helped me investigate the murder I'd been accused of.

"You want to be my date tonight?" he asked.

"Are you taking me to the opera?"

"Nope."

"Are you taking me to a hoity-toity restaurant, where they blindfold you and make you listen to crashing waves while they serve you microscopic portions of food?"

"Wrong again."

"Then you must be taking me to the bar at the Old Mill, so the answer is obviously yes."

"Actually, the Old Mill will have to wait. I'm taking you to a garden party."

"A garden party?"

"See, there's this guy, Barry Longo, who's a financial adviser—"

"Wait, we're going to a financial adviser's garden party?" I put my hands on my hips. "Who are you, and what have you done with Nat?"

Nat grinned. "You love a mystery. So I'm making sure we keep our friendship interesting. You ready to go?"

It took me another 15 minutes to sweep up and put the cash in the safe—a new and important part of the closing routine. I reminded Angelica to bolt the back door. The security camera still needed to be replaced out back, and I was paranoid that, in the interim, we were leaving the bakery vulnerable. But Angelica waved me away.

"Chief Tedesco said burglars rarely strike a second time," she said, as careless as if the break-in had never happened. "Go have fun."

Outside, I got into Nat's car, an old Honda Accord with dancing bear stickers on the back and a pair of tie-dye dice hanging from the rearview mirror. As he swung into traffic on Garibaldi Avenue, I expressed my amazement at Angelica's quick recovery.

"I swear that if a tsunami washed over Carmine, she would find something positive to say about it."

"The water would be good for the flowers and lawns," Nat suggested.

"So tell me about this guy and why we're going to his garden party."

We drove down Garibaldi Avenue, Carmine's main street, and Nat turned left, steering us away from the stores and into a residential neighborhood.

"Barry Longo's his name," Nat said. "He's an independent financial adviser. The word around town is that he's made people a lot of money."

"As soon as someone says that, it's usually a sign they're shady."

"True. But Dan Russo has invested with him, and insists the returns have been amazing."

Dan Russo of Russo's Realty seemed like a reliable guy. He headed up the Chamber of Commerce with Joanna Parisi and Angelica.

"If Dan vouches for the guy, maybe he's OK," I said. "But why do you care? Do you have savings you want to invest?"

"Savings?" Nat laughed. "That's the funniest thing you've said in ages. No, I'm going because of work. The Carmine Historical Society is struggling. We're short on funds and need more donors. I'm hoping to talk Barry into giving."

We drove through Cedar Hill, where the richest people lived in beautiful—and massive—Victorian mansions. The neighborhood we passed into next, though not as fancy, worked hard to show its wealth. Many houses reached above the trees in the yards. They were multi-story homes with three- or even four-car garages. The gardeners must use nail clippers to manicure the perfectly trimmed lawns.

A white picket fence surrounded one property. Wrought-iron bars ringed another, giving it a castle-like feel.

We pulled up in front of that property.

"Wow," I said.

"There's no other word for it," Nat agreed.

Barry Longo's home outdid most of the neighbors. It was a real McMansion. Neoclassical columns supported a massive double-door entrance. The windows on either side were taller than my own home and featured stained glass. Multiple gables interrupted the roofline, giving the impression that the house was a small village scrunched into a single building.

We got out of the car and walked through the gothic iron gate. It would have made Dracula proud. Fake gas lamps lined the stone path leading to the front door. Yet the garden was a cheerful explosion of flowers and plants—it seemed to aspire to Hawaiian abundance instead of Transylvanian gloom.

The garden party was well under way. Long tables heaped with food and drinks fronted a thicket of plants: a variety of roses, interspersed with purple, bell-like flowers. A sycamore tree, with its dappled bark, cast shade across the lawn.

At the tables stood catering staff, most of them teenagers in matching t-shirts.

Guests milled around with drinks—glasses of wine, beer bottles, and cocktails—and their conversation competed with a sound system pumping out loud top 40 hits.

A woman approached us, a glass of white wine in her hand.

"Aren't you Bernadette Kovac?"

"I go by Bernie Smyth now."

She wasn't listening. "I loved you on *Silver & Gold,*

Bernadette. Fabulous show. Absolutely fabulous. Shame about Jay Casanova. But *c'est la vie*, right? Oh, is that you over there, Jennie darling? What an adorable dress. Adorable."

She drifted off again.

I sighed. This wasn't my kind of shindig. It reminded me too much of the parties in Hollywood hosted by producers or directors or famous actors, like my *Silver & Gold* co-star, Jay Casanova. Lots of people name-dropping and pretending to have a good time wasn't my idea of fun.

"It's ridiculous," Nat agreed, when I shared my feelings. "But we're not trying to impress anyone. Let's see if Barry Longo has a heart of gold and wants to support the historical society, or at least wants a big tax write-off. Then we can go to the Old Mill and laugh about it all. In the meantime, why not have fun?"

"At parties like this, only the people skinning other people are having a good time."

"Well, hello, Ms. Cynical."

We got drinks at one of the catering stations. The white tablecloth had a logo printed on it, the same as on the t-shirts worn by the staff: a fluffy cloud with the words "Italian Dream" floating inside.

We both got beers.

As we turned around to survey the party, I caught sight of Anthony. Now, what was he doing here? Unsurprisingly, he was speaking—or rather flirting—with an attractive twenty-something woman. She must be a decade younger than Anthony, who, like me, was in his early thirties.

"Does it bother you?" Nat asked me, apparently guessing what I was looking at.

I gave it some serious thought. No, it didn't bother me. I explained to Nat that I was done with Anthony, completely over him, though I found the aftermath of our brief relationship half-annoying, half-interesting.

"So you don't hate him for what he did?" Nat asked.

"Hate? Jeez, that's a strong word."

"Love, death, and money—those three things can make people hate like nothing else."

"Anthony got me miffed. But he and I would never have worked out, anyway. Since I never loved him, I could never hate him."

"Speaking of love and hate," Nat said, nodding at someone to our left.

Turning, I caught sight of Crystal Alfano with an older man. Crystal, who'd gone to high school with Nat, had married Angelica's middle-aged ex-husband and was now pregnant with their child.

"Is that Marty with her?"

"The man himself," Nat confirmed.

I'd never seen Marty Alfano before, yet I already considered him a *disgraziad*. He'd broken Angelica's heart and cheated on her with young Crystal, eventually moving with her to Short Hills, New Jersey. In his late forties, he'd gone mostly bald, but a border of black hair still clung to the sides of his head. He had a thick salt-and-pepper mustache. He wore loafers, chinos, and a white button-down shirt, open at the neck—a simplicity to his style that somehow underscored how wealthy he must be.

Crystal, standing by his side, had one hand on her pregnant belly. The other held a glass of water. Her mouth was turned down in a frown and she stared off into the middle distance, as if her mind was far away—or wished it were.

Marty was talking to another man, roughly late forties as well, with dark, curly hair, a long nose, and full lips. The guy wore an aloha shirt—blue with pink flamingos.

"That's Barry Longo," Nat explained.

"And that's a shirt," I said.

"The man stands out."

It was true. Barry was a bright spot in a field of beige, camel, and pastel. I recognized other people at the party: Dan Russo, Carmine's premier realtor, head of the chamber of commerce, and friend of Angelica's. Joanna Parisi of Parisi & Parisi, Attorneys at Law, which she shared with her husband, Gino Parisi, who was perennially absent. I also spotted Mayor Tom Blink, who was wolfing down a lobster roll.

Then, as a familiar face emerged from the crowd, I gaped.

"Angelica? What are you doing here?"

Angelica laughed. "I'm surprised I'm here, too. Dan and Joanna convinced me at the last minute. And why not? Maybe I should be thinking about how to invest some of my earnings from the bakery."

Why not? I could tell her why not, and he was standing ten paces behind her: Marty Alfano. As far as I knew, the two weren't on speaking terms, and I didn't want to see Angelica get hurt again by him. Marty Alfano was bad news. How Angelica and he had ever been married was a big mystery to me.

Angelica must have seen me staring at Marty across her shoulder. She half-turned, saw him, and then put a hand on my cheek.

"*Mia cara,* you worry too much about me. I've put my divorce behind me. Crystal and I have become friends. Maybe someday Marty and I can..." She sighed. "When Marty and I separated, it was a bitter experience, but time passes. Wounds heal. These days, I would do anything to put that behind us and find a way to be friendly, if not friends."

I wondered whether Marty would say the same. But I didn't ask Angelica about that. I smiled and suggested we get another drink.

"And let's get some food," Nat suggested. "I'm getting hungry watching Mayor Blink eat all those lobster rolls."

After getting Angelica a glass of white wine, we approached the catering stations. The array of foods was impressive.

A charcuterie and cheese platter included prosciutto, salami, and coppa, along with half a dozen hard and soft cheeses, crackers, and bread. There was a carving station with beef tenderloin and turkey. Gourmet canapés of smoked salmon with crème fraîche on crostini and mini quiches dotted platters. Half a dozen dips ringed a gargantuan platter overflowing with raw vegetables—cauliflower, carrots, cucumbers, and so much more.

"Ooh," Angelica said. "There's a dessert station, too."

Tiered cookie stands held chocolate truffles, mini fruit tarts, as well as an assortment of cookies. There was a platter with crème brûlée and another with small cream-filled cakes.

"Please take anything you want," the woman behind the table said. "And if I can be helpful, just let me know."

Unlike the other staff members, she was in her thirties. Blonde. Red lipstick. She wore an apron that said "Italian Dream," the letters stretching across her ample chest.

"These are delicious," Angelica said. She was sampling one of the cream-filled cakes.

"So are these," Nat added, as he bit into a lobster roll.

"Who doesn't love lobster?" the woman said with a wink. "Have you tried the blini?"

If she was flirting with Nat, she wouldn't get far, since he didn't date women.

"Is this your catering company?" I asked her.

She nodded. "I do all of Barry's parties."

Instinctively, I looked down at her hands. She wore no ring.

"Are you his—?"

She winced. "Everyone asks that. I'm his sister, and believe me, he benefits from a big family discount. But my business depends on connections, meeting the right people, word of mouth."

She introduced herself as Betsy Longo.

"I know who you are, of course," she told me.

"Eve Silver," I said, anticipating her comment.

"Sure. But you're also the one who caught Johnny Greco's killer."

By now, everyone in Carmine knew I wasn't simply Bernie Smyth, baking assistant, but also the actress Bernadette Kovac, who'd played Eve Silver on *Silver & Gold*. Apparently, my reputation as an amateur sleuth was also spreading.

"It was nothing," I mumbled, suddenly wishing she'd only wanted to talk about Eve Silver. I still felt uncomfortable talking about my sleuthing. After all, I wasn't a real detective, just someone who couldn't leave a mystery well enough alone. In fact, it was a compulsion.

Nat came to my rescue. He asked Betsy about the different foods—the lobster rolls, the tenderloin, the salad bar—while I gazed into the distance, dreaming about the long, strange trip that had led me from Hollywood actress to bakery assistant and amateur sleuth in Carmine.

As I came out of my daydream, my eyes focused on a truck in the street.

A USPS mail truck.

It drifted past, but I could not see the driver inside. Then it turned down a side street, vanishing.

I shook my head.

Impossible.

U.S. Marshall Roberta LaRosa, my point of contact in witness protection, had shown up in a mail truck whenever she wanted to make contact. After I left the program, she'd vanished from my life. But I missed her sudden appearances and disappearances.

The mail truck, however, could only have been a mail truck. There was no reason for Roberta to return to Carmine.

AS THE PARTY DRAGGED ON, the sun sank over the giant houses. The sycamore cast a long shadow. As the day dimmed, the guests grew louder, hand gestures more expressive, and laughter more open-mouthed. Someone turned up the music to compete with the conversations.

I'd made the mistake of standing near the sound system. The speakers roared. The bass thumped harder and harder, rumbling in my gut like an earth tremor.

A couple of women guzzling white wine stood next to me, yelling happily at each other and leaning closer and closer.

"I made fifty grand in 24 hours."

"That's nothing," the other said. "After my first round, I got back 100k."

"You reinvested, right?"

"Oh, you'd better believe it." She laughed. "Though I kept a cool five thousand for shopping."

Near the dessert station, Nat frowned at a man in a salmon sports coat who was explaining the magic of mutual funds. I thanked my lucky stars that I'd kept out of those conversations. Despite the noise of the music, I'd found myself a secluded spot between the sound system and the rose bushes.

I sipped my lukewarm IPA and watched the party. I was reflecting on why people bothered to drink warm beer when the music stopped.

It was so sudden that it sent a jolt through me, like stepping off a moving treadmill to solid, motionless ground.

"That's enough, Barry," a voice said.

A man was standing on the other side of the sound system. I knew him. It was Phil Palladino. About 60 years old, he wore corduroy pants and a knitted cardigan. He was bald, but I happened to know that he'd once had an abundance of permed hair. That was back in the 1980s, when he'd belonged to the hair metal band Tarantella. These days he ran Milano Books on Garibaldi Avenue.

"Come join the party, Phil," Barry Longo said, sauntering over to the newcomer. He smiled. "Instead of worrying about the music, you should enjoy it. Come have a drink."

He raised his cocktail and shook it so that the ice cubes tinkled against the glass.

"Thank you, I'd rather not." Phil crossed his arms. "The music is ear deafening."

Barry called out his sister's name. "Come on, Betsy, get my friend a glass of white wine. Can't you see the man needs a drink?"

Phil ignored the offer. "Barry, you said last time you'd keep the noise down, and the time before that."

Marty pushed his way through the crowd, joining Barry.

"What's the problem? Why'd you turn off the music?"

"This has nothing to do with you, Marty," Phil said.

"What if we play Tarantella? Maybe then you'll like the music better."

A few guests snickered.

Phil ignored them. He ignored Marty, too.

He told Barry, "I'll call the cops, if I have to."

"No, no." Barry held up his hands to placate Phil, the ice in his drink jiggling. "There's no need to call the cops. No need for that."

Marty stepped forward and jabbed a finger at Phil.

"Go home and knit a sweater, little man. Leave us big boys to party."

Phil shook his head. "Some day, Marty, your attitude is going to get you into trouble."

Marty smirked. "My attitude has made me millions. I'm not the loser here."

Phil turned away, muttering something under his breath as he headed for the gate.

Phil had walked halfway down the sidewalk to his own modest house next door when Marty turned the music back on, cranking it even louder. But Barry stepped in and lowered the volume.

"Take it easy, Marty."

Barry put a hand on Marty's arm and leaned close, apparently wanting their words to be private.

But partly hidden behind the sound system, I could still hear them.

"Let's not bring the cops down on our heads," Barry said.

"The cops make you nervous, do they?" Marty smiled. It was a nasty smile, like he enjoyed sticking a knife into Barry. "When the cops come, Mr. Money Bags, it will not be because the music is too loud."

Marty moved off to the bar, leaving Barry with a frown on his face.

"Wait a sec, Marty..."

Barry set his cocktail glass down on one of the speakers, and drawing in a deep breath, he ran a hand across his forehead. He gazed after Marty, who was weaving in and out of the crowd, and then exhaled.

"Hold on, Marty, let's talk..." he called out as he followed Marty into the crowd.

I watched the two men disappear.

Hmm...

Why would the police make Barry nervous? What was this about the cops coming for him?

Marty and Barry shared some kind of secret, but what was it?

A familiar fluttering in my belly warned me I'd better follow them—here was a mystery I couldn't leave alone. If I didn't get answers to my questions, I would be pacing my bedroom all night wondering about them. I set down my bottle of beer on the speaker, right next to Barry's abandoned drink.

Marty had slipped out of sight. I scanned the crowd for him. In a sea of men in chinos and white button-downs, I caught hold of a man's shoulder, but as he turned, I saw he had a full head of hair.

"Sorry," I murmured and slipped past him.

A flash of blue and pink caught my eye. Nothing subtle about that shirt. Barry bounded up the steps to the house and vanished inside.

Maybe he was following Marty.

A moment later, I was inside the cool interior. The foyer was massive. A staircase flanked its sides and rose to landings on the second and third floors. High above, the ceiling stretched into a kind of triangle of light. I shielded my eyes, and peering through the glare, I saw it was a skylight shaped like a glass pyramid, and within it was the stained-glass pattern of an eye. Like the pyramid and eye on the dollar bill.

Classy.

So, where had Barry gone—upstairs or downstairs?

Ahead of me, the foyer branched off, and I could hear the clink of glasses and the whirring sound of an appliance, presumably from the kitchen. An open doorway to the left led to a banquet-sized dining room. Across from it, I made out an equally massive den with multiple sofa sets and a huge widescreen TV that belonged in a movie theater.

But no Barry.

Before anyone could catch me, I grabbed the banister and tiptoed up the stairs.

The stairs were wooden, yet didn't creak. Maybe that was a sign of true wealth: stairs that didn't creak. In any case, it was every amateur sleuth's dream.

I got to the first landing. Every door was closed. I leaned against the first, listening. Careful not to make too much noise, I turned the door handle. The door eased open. Inside was a workout room with a running machine, an elliptical, and a rowing machine, plus all kinds of weights. Another gigantic TV screen, too.

I closed the door and checked the next. This was a closet the size of my bedroom. The next door led to an actual bedroom, with a four-poster bed, a small desk, and plenty of built-in closets. Everything was sparse, immaculate, and untouched in a way that suggested a guest room.

I was backing out, closing the door, when someone said,

"Can I help you?"

I froze. "Uh..."

"Are you lost?"

One of the Italian Dream staff was eyeing me. She was in her late teens, I guessed, with a shaved head, a row of earrings lining one lobe, and purple lipstick. She didn't look like she belonged in her Italian Dream t-shirt, let alone among the moneyed people at Barry's party. My guess was that, in her spare time, she wore heavy black boots, ripped jeans, and t-shirts with the names of goth or death metal bands slashed across the front in bloody lettering.

"Yes, I'm lost," I said, trying to think of an excuse.

"Are you looking for the restroom?"

"That's right," I said, grabbing onto the excuse she'd provided me with. "The restroom. I desperately need to go."

"There's one downstairs, but it's pretty busy. I've been using the one up here."

She stuck out her thumb and gestured at a door at the other end of the landing. Then grabbed her left arm with her right.

"You're Bernie Smyth." She bit her lip. "I recognize you from the news...and from Moroni's..."

Her name was Lily, she told me, and there was something she wanted to ask me. But apparently it made her awkward. I waited for her to say what was on her mind, hoping it had nothing to do with me snooping in Barry's home.

"The thing is that my big dream—well, it's becoming a baker. I already do a lot of baking by myself, and I've learned a little at Italian Dream. But I was wondering..."

She trailed off, looking down at her feet.

Whatever made her so awkward, it was going to take a lifetime for her to get the words out. The longer this went on, the less likely it was that I'd find Barry and Marty. I glanced over my shoulder at the door, hoping she got the hint.

"Oh, you need the restroom," she said. "Of course, sorry. Stupid me."

"I'll find you outside, and we can talk."

"OK. Cool."

Lily turned, her shoulders sagging, and she descended the stairs one slow step at a time.

I slipped into the restroom. I would have to hide for a minute, then continue my search once I was sure she was gone.

The bathroom, like the rest of the house, was oversized. A large window stood open, the balmy breeze blowing in. There was a bath, a separate shower stall, and two toilets. I studied the setup for a moment, wondering whether it encouraged socializing on the potty. While I was trying to make sense of it, I heard voices from outside.

I moved to the window. I had a view of a backyard, its long lawn sloping down to the iron fence dividing Barry's property from the next. The party was on the other side of the house and the sound of music was distant. Leaning out, I could see a patio right below me. A bald man stood there— Marty Alfano—talking to someone. But an awning jutted out from the house and obscured the other person.

"I said all there is to say." Marty flicked a hand at the other person. A dismissive gesture. "Don't push me."

A murmured response. The other voice was too low for me to make out. Was it a man or a woman?

"Are you threatening me?" Marty said. "Don't think for a moment that I'm afraid of you."

Another pause from Marty as the other person murmured a response.

Marty laughed. "You're crazy."

Footsteps sounded on the stone tiles—whoever Marty had faced was walking away.

Marty put his hands in his pockets, and shaking his head, dug out a cigar. He flicked open a Zippo lighter and puffed on the cigar until it smoked and then chuckled to himself. He dug out his phone and scrolled, vanishing under the awning as he did so. He must be returning to the party.

I pulled back into the bathroom and leaned against the windowsill.

Who had Marty been talking to? They must have met behind the house because it was secluded and private—there would be no one else around to overhear their conversation. Which meant they knew each other. Why else would Marty meet the person in private? I wish I could have heard the other person's voice. Could it have been Barry? Whoever it was, the person had threatened Marty.

I hurried downstairs and slipped through the front door. The air conditioning had made the house cool. Outside, the humid air hit me like a wave.

Standing on the porch, I got a good view of the party. I scanned the crowd to find Marty. Maybe he'd followed the person he'd talked to. Or they'd continued their conversation elsewhere.

I saw no sign of Barry's bright shirt. Nat stood at a food station, having escaped the conversation about mutual funds, and he was pointing at a platter with sliders. Lily, the girl I'd met inside, leaned over and grabbed one of the mini hamburgers and put it on a plate for him. Over by the bar, Dan Russo and Joanna Parisi were talking to Crystal. Mayor Blink hovered nearby, a glass of red in one hand, a meat skewer in the other.

Then I saw Marty.

He stood near the sound system, the speakers yet again thumping loudly. He leaned close to his companion—because of the noise, perhaps, or because of the intimacy of their conversation—and when I saw who he was speaking with, my heart skipped a beat.

It was Angelica.

As I watched, she put a hand on Marty's arm and smiled.

Marty, cigar jutting out of the corner of his mouth, stared down at the hand with narrowed eyes. Then shook it off and turned away.

FRIDAY MORNING, I put up a colorful sign in Moroni's front window. It advertised the partnership between the bakery and "Carmine's favorite Italian restaurant" to cater the Italian Day Celebration next Saturday, inviting townsfolk and their friends and relatives to join the festivities. Carlo had put up a similar one in his window next door. The message was ringed with Italian flags, and quaint illustrations of fusilli pasta and cannolis dotted the poster.

I was admiring the sign from the outside when I caught sight of an envelope on the doorstep.

I went inside and handed it to Angelica.

"We must have walked right over it when we opened this morning," she said.

It was white. No stamp. Her name was written in block letters on the front.

Standing behind the counter, she tore it open and pulled out a simple blank card. At least it was blank on the side I could see. I watched Angelica's eyes darting back and forth as she read the note.

"Who's it from?" I asked, curious. "What does it say?"

Angelica stood behind the counter, studying the message.

Her eyes sparkled with excitement. "I can't tell you."

"You can't what?" I crossed my arms and frowned, giving her a stern look. "First, you refuse to give me the skinny on your conversation with Marty—"

"I told you yesterday that it wasn't me talking to him in the backyard, and that when we spoke, it was mostly me trying to show I was willing to let bygones be bygones."

"—and now you're being downright mysterious about this mystery note."

"I'll tell you everything tomorrow. Promise."

And with that, she folded the note in half, turned on her heels, and headed through the back door and into her little office. Standing in the doorway to the café, I spied on her. She was pinning the folded note to her corkboard, right next to the little hook where she usually hung the extra set of keys.

A knot twisted my stomach. I had a bad feeling this was related to her encounter with Marty. What if he were toying with her, setting her up for more heartbreak? I couldn't let him hurt her again.

As she emerged from the office, I blocked the passage, hands on my hips.

"Does this have anything to do with Marty?" I asked.

"Wait until tomorrow." She raised a finger, wagging it at me. "And no snooping, detective."

She got back to work in the bakery. There was a bounce to her step, and she started whistling a cheerful tune. As she spread flour across the workspace, she asked me if I could open the bakery and handle customers—she needed to bake an extra batch of cookies.

After serving the first few customers—Joanna Parisi and

Dan Russo, who wanted their favorite coffees before heading to the office—I returned to the bakery and leaned against the doorway to watch Angelica work. Next to her, on the countertop, stood jars of sugar and cocoa powder and flour, as well as a bag of almonds and a tub of honey.

"What are you making?" I asked.

"Cookies."

"What kinds of cookies?"

She paused. "I guess I'm not giving away any secrets. I'm making Neapolitan *mustaccioli.*"

I'd never heard of mustaccioli before. Angelica turned her attention to her work again, making it clear she wouldn't give me any more clues.

Anyway, at that moment, the little bell over the front door jingled softly, calling me away.

I hurried back to the counter.

"Morning," Nat said with a smile.

I snuck around the counter and motioned for Nat to sit down with me at a table. We leaned close so I could whisper. I told him about the mysterious note and Angelica's sudden need to bake an extra batch of cookies.

He flipped his fringe of hair out of his face.

"A mystery..."

He sounded pleased.

"I bet the cookies are for the sender of the note," I said. "But all she'll tell me is that she's making Neapolitan mustaccioli, whatever they are."

Nat googled the name on his phone.

"Check it out."

He showed me a picture of rhombus-shaped, chocolate-covered cookies.

"They look quite familiar," I said. "What's special about them?"

"Well, for one thing, they're typical Christmas cookies."

"That's why I haven't seen Angelica make them yet. She mostly sticks to the seasons."

Angelica appeared in the doorway, and Nat and I looked up with the innocence of cats caught rummaging in the pantry. But Angelica didn't seem to notice. She was distracted.

"Bernie, have you seen my notebook?"

"Notebook?"

"The thick one I keep in my office next to the computer."

I shook my head.

"That's strange. I must have brought it home and forgot."

"What's the notebook for?" Nat asked.

"Many years ago, I went to Italy to study baking, and I kept a journal. The notebook contains all the old recipes I picked up during my trip, including my favorite mustaccioli recipe. But it's no problem—I think I can remember all the ingredients."

She returned to the bakery.

Nat sat hunched over his phone for a while, searching for something and watching videos.

"Here, look at this."

He showed me a video of a food vlogger who visited an Italian bakery in New York City.

"See what she's eating?"

"Mustaccioli. But so what?"

"Right now, Italian cookies are trending. My theory is this: Angelica has a rendezvous with a food critic."

"She's acting as if she has a rendezvous with the CIA."

"That's the thing. Some of these critics are very secretive. They often show up when you least expect it, and there's one guy—he's old school, not even on social media—who'll wear disguises to make sure people don't give him special treatment."

I was skeptical. "I don't know, Nat. I know the bakery is close to Angelica's heart, but this feels more personal than getting a food critic to visit."

I shared my worries about Marty messing with Angelica's feelings, and Nat rubbed his chin, looking thoughtful. "Maybe. But I can't believe she'd fall for his charm again."

"Charm?" I laughed. "Don't be funny. The guy's awful."

"True, but he can be charming when he wants to, especially around women."

For a while, we watched videos of top food critics. Several covered the mustaccioli cookies from a particular bakery in New York City, Vitale's Cookies. The youngest vlogger, Jacky Yu, had a funny, direct style, where she filmed herself selfie-style as she tasted things in the bakery. Her reactions were often exaggerated, her language colorful. She was truly entertaining—I recognized show biz talent when I saw it.

Occasionally, I had to get up to serve a customer. Nat glanced at the time and admitted that he ought to get to work. "But playing hooky with you is much more fun."

"It's about to get even more fun," Angelica said from the doorway to the back.

She held out a tray of chocolate-covered cookies. Now I knew what they were: mustaccioli.

"Try them," she urged us as she came to our table and set down the tray.

I bit into one of the cookies. My teeth sank into the soft chocolate exterior. Then crunched into ground almonds inside. A delicate zest of orange spread through my mouth, as did cinnamon and cloves, and I closed my eyes. Once again, Angelica's baking had the magic ability to send my mind—even my whole body—to a better place.

"Amazing," I said with a sigh.

"Yum," Nat agreed. "I won't say not to seconds."

"Oh no, you don't." Angelica playfully slapped Nat's hand away. "I'm saving the rest. My friend will get them as a morning treat with a cup of coffee."

"Your friend?" Nat said, trying to sound innocent. "And who is this friend?"

"Don't try to fool me, Nat. I know you and Bernie are in cahoots. I'm telling no one."

And with that, she removed the tray and set it on the counter behind the cash register. She told me she'd be right back, and would I mind managing the café for a while longer?

I said, "No problem."

There were no customers, so Nat and I watched another video—this one about pizzelles. An ad interrupted the video, a commercial for investing money in stocks, which reminded me of the garden party.

"Did you have any luck getting Barry to donate money to the historical society?"

He shook his head. "The guy said he already gave plenty to charities, but when I asked him which ones, he got defensive. 'It's my money,' he told me. 'I put it where I want it.'"

"He doesn't sound like much of a philanthropist."

We watched another of Jacky Yu's videos about food. This time she was tasting cannolis at a place in Brooklyn. In the next, she interviewed a fellow critic, a middle-aged man with short salt-and-pepper hair.

"That's George Pullman," Nat said, "the guy I was telling you about who wears disguises."

"I bet these food critics would love Moroni's," I said.

"No doubt about it."

Nat grew thoughtful. He muttered to himself, "Yeah, there's no doubt about it. No doubt whatsoever."

After Nat left for work, I tidied up. I ripped open a roll of quarters and added the change to the cash register. A customer came, and I sold him some pignoli cookies. Another came to get a latte to go. Then it grew quiet again.

I drifted back to the bakery, where Angelica was busy scrubbing a pan.

I turned and glanced back at the open office door—and at the mysterious note.

Checking that Angelica was still busy, I tiptoed into the office.

There was the note, neatly folded and pegged to the corkboard.

Angelica had made it clear she didn't want anyone to read it. She'd asked me not to snoop. But by tomorrow, the secret would no longer be a secret, and it made my whole body itch to see the note and do nothing. It was like a hundred ants were crawling all over me. I couldn't concentrate, and if I couldn't concentrate, how could I be a good employee? In fact, by clearing up this little mystery, I told myself, I'd be helping myself get more work done, which meant helping Moroni's.

And isn't that the most important thing to Angelica?

I sighed. A better person wouldn't believe that kind of logic. A better person would stay away.

"Good thing I'm imperfect," I muttered to myself as I gently pried the note off the board.

I unfolded the stiff paper.

My dear Angelica, it was such a pleasure to see you at the garden party. I want to see you again. There is a serious matter I would like your help with. It's about my fatherhood. Nothing would make me happier than to talk it over while drinking coffee and eating my favorite cookie with you. Would you mind baking a batch? For old times' sake?

I'll drop by Moroni's tomorrow at 6:30 am, so I can catch you before we both have to work.

Please don't tell anyone, not even your closest friends or family—I don't want this to get back to Crystal, who wouldn't understand.

Warmly, Marty.

Why did Marty suddenly want to reestablish relations with Angelica? What "serious matter about fatherhood" did he want her advice on? And why so secretive about it?

I could understand why Crystal might be suspicious if she found out Marty was meeting with other women, but Angelica and Crystal had forged a friendship. They hadn't advertised it, but surely Marty knew.

No, Marty must have some other reason. I worried his reasons weren't honorable. He'd certainly played on Angelica's weakness by asking her to help him with being a father. Since it might affect the child's future happiness, how could Angelica resist such a request?

I pinned the note back on the board, making sure it was

precisely where I'd found it, next to the hook for the extra keys.

As I got back to work, too many questions lingered. Sure, the ants plaguing me about the note were gone, but I'd replaced them with a swarm of butterflies in my gut, an uneasy feeling that whatever Marty wanted with Angelica, it wasn't good.

I tried to focus on work instead. I made myself an espresso. It didn't make me feel any better, only more jittery.

Calm down. Tomorrow, Bernie, all this will be resolved. Tomorrow you'll find out.

If there was one thing I was lousy at, it was waiting.

THE NEXT MORNING, I left my little house on Lampedusa Lane, and, stepping out of the front door, froze. A police cruiser stood parked in my driveway.

Had something happened?

The window rolled down, revealing Chief Tedesco. She had her sunglasses on against the bright sunlight.

"I'm going to drop by Moroni's to check in on Angelica," she explained. "It's really an excuse to grab a decent cup of coffee. Jump in. I'll give you a ride."

With a sigh of relief, I got into the passenger seat. A moment later, we were rolling down Lampedusa and turning onto Da Vinci Street. A kid threw a Frisbee across her front yard, and her black labrador puppy chased it. In front of a ranch-style home like mine, a woman in a suit was getting into her car, while her husband, baby on his hip, stood in the doorway and waved goodbye. A man clad in cycling shorts whizzed past us on a racing bike, his head stretched over the handlebars as his legs pumped the pedals.

It was another sunny morning in Carmine.

Moroni's, halfway down Garibaldi Avenue, wasn't far, and on a day like this, with blue skies and no threat of rain, I would have relished the morning walk. But Chief Tedesco never offered me a ride to work. I guessed she wanted to talk.

"Any new leads on the break-in?" I asked.

She shook her head. "Carlo's security camera caught nothing. No witnesses have come forward. They left no prints, and the bakery is such a jumble of DNA traces that we got nothing concrete. If they'd stolen something easy to trace, we might have a chance at catching them. But as it is, I'm afraid it's like so many burglaries—it'll remain unsolved. How's Angelica coping?"

"Angelica is already over it," I said.

"And you?"

"I'm fine."

A lie. Every morning, I arrived at work and expected to find the bakery in disarray, and it wasn't until I'd stepped inside and made sure that everything was all right that the knot of worry in my stomach untangled.

"Another thing, Bernie. Have you seen U.S. Marshall Roberta LaRosa recently?"

I studied Tedesco's face. Behind her sunglasses, her expression was impossible to read.

"Maybe," I said. "Maybe not. Why?"

"Not sure. I think I may have seen her, and the first time, I assumed she was visiting you..."

"The first time? You've seen her more than once?"

"Either that or every USPS mail truck makes me suspicious." She laughed. "In fact, that's probably it. I've become delusional and think every mail truck is driven by a U.S. Marshall."

I smiled. That was how I felt. Surely, I hadn't seen Roberta drive past Barry Longo's garden party. But the fact that Chief Tedesco also thought she'd spotted the U.S. Marshall increased my suspicions. If Roberta was in town, why hadn't she visited me? Why so secretive?

We pulled up to Moroni's, and both got out of the cruiser. Chief Tedesco slipped off her sunglasses as I dug out my keys. Angelica would have arrived already, and she'd be busy in the backroom bakery. We usually kept the front door locked until we officially opened for the day.

I put my key in the lock, turned, and then pulled open the door.

Inside the café, a man sat hunched over one of the tables. Music played from the speakers mounted in the four corners of the tin ceiling: the Andrews Sisters sang about shortening bread. The man, I realized, didn't move—he was slumped over the table, as if passed out.

For a moment, Chief Tedesco and I stood in the entrance, frozen.

Angelica came through the doorway at the back, wiping her hands on a cloth, humming along to the music.

She stopped too.

"Marty?"

Angelica's voice seemed to wake Chief Tedesco. She pushed past me.

She bent over Marty—I recognized his bald head—and put a hand on his neck.

"No pulse. He's not breathing, either."

Angelica gasped. "No."

"Yes." Chief Tedesco glanced at Angelica, then over at me, a frown forming on her face. "Marty's dead."

3

The interior of Carlo's Restaurant was designed to mute loud sounds: carpeted floors, heavy drapes, even acoustic paneling in the ceiling. A soundtrack of soft jazz played on repeat.

In contrast, Carlo, Angelica's brother, bustled out of the kitchen, his arms loaded with a serving platter, wine glasses threaded through his fingers, and two bottles, one shoved under each bicep.

"Please, eat—*mangia, mangia,*" he said, setting the platter down, then the glasses, and finally the bottles.

He'd heaped the platter with antipasti: salami and prosciutto, marinated artichokes, olives, and peppers, slices of fresh mozzarella and pecorino. He'd brought two bottles of wine, one white and one red.

Angelica and I, hardly hungry at such an early hour, pecked at the food.

Carlo scratched his goatee.

"You're not eating. *Madone,* it's the stress."

"Carlo," Angelica said. "Please. The stress I'm feeling is because you can't sit still."

"Sorry, *mia cara*."

He pulled out a chair and sat down, which accentuated his potbelly. But he'd only sat for a few seconds when he slapped his forehead. He shot to his feet and rushed back to the kitchen, the door swinging shut behind him. Before the door had settled, he thrust it open and came charging back with a basket full of crusty bread and a tray with dipping bowls.

"I almost forgot the olive oil for dipping," he said.

He sat down again and watched us anxiously.

Angelica grabbed a piece of bread, broke off a hunk, and dipped it in oil.

"Good." Carlo nodded encouragingly. "It's good, isn't it?"

I had a piece of bread with oil, too, and Carlo was right: it was good. The olive oil, which he imported specially from a farm in Sicily, had a strong pepperiness to it.

"I can't believe it..." Angelica said, clearly searching for words to make sense of what had happened.

"Do you think Marty could have had a heart attack?" I asked.

"It's possible. One minute he was fine, eating the cookies and drinking coffee, the next I see Chief Tedesco standing over his lifeless body."

"Here, try some artichoke," Carlo said, turning the platter to make it easy for Angelica to reach it.

We nibbled artichoke and salami and slices of mozzarella, and with every bite, I felt my hunger increase. Carlo had been right to treat our shock with Italian food. It gave us the strength to talk about Marty and his death. He served us glasses of red wine and we drank. In my experience, there was no shame in drinking in the morning when you'd found a dead body.

By the time we'd gone back over the details a half-dozen

times, the front door to the restaurant opened and Chief Tedesco walked in.

She pulled over a chair from another table, flipping it around, so she could rest her arms on its back. Shadows had gathered around her eyes. She pinched her nose, and I guessed by the way she winced that she had a bad headache.

The three of us—Angelica, Carlo, and me—waited for her to speak.

"Marty's death was no accident," she said.

Angelica gasped.

"So it wasn't a heart attack?" I said.

"He was probably poisoned. The coroner is pretty sure, but we'll only know for sure once we get the full autopsy."

"Poisoned?" I asked.

Chief Tedesco glanced at Angelica before answering me. "Yes, poisoned. Forensics have taken samples of the cookies as well as all dry and wet ingredients Angelica used to make the cookies and sent them off to the lab, but it can take a while to get the full results."

Angelica turned pale. "Are you saying my cookies killed Marty?"

"Until we get the results from the lab, we won't know. Did anyone help you make the cookies or come near the ingredients?"

She shook her head. "I didn't even let Bernie help."

"I see."

I cut in. "How could Marty have been poisoned by Angelica's cookies? She ate one herself, and so did Nat and I. None of us are dead. There's got to be another explanation."

Chief Tedesco nodded. "I agree. But the facts are these: at the time of Marty's death, the front and back doors were both locked, Marty sat in the café drinking coffee and eating cookies, and Angelica was the only other person inside Moroni's when you and I arrived."

"Someone must have known Marty was coming and set the whole thing up."

"That's a pretty elaborate theory, Bernie." Chief Tedesco pursed her lips, momentarily lost in thought. "All right, let's pursue your idea for a moment. Who else knew Marty was coming, Angelica?"

"I didn't tell anyone. Not even Bernie knew."

I bit the inside of my cheek and did my best to look innocent. I did know, of course, because I had peeked at the card she'd stuck to the corkboard.

"And did Marty tell anyone?" Chief Tedesco asked.

Angelica looked thoughtful. "He said he hadn't told Crystal, and I don't know who else he would have told. He acted strangely, though, like he was suspicious about my intentions. Which made no sense, since he was the one who'd invited himself over."

"You'd better come down to the station so we can get a full statement."

"I understand," Angelica said, picking up her glass, taking one last sip. "Bernie, will you look after the bakery while I'm gone?"

"I'd be happy to, and I'll—"

"I'm sorry, Angelica," Chief Tedesco cut in, "but until we get the results from the autopsy and the lab, the bakery is a crime scene. That means we'll have to close it."

"Close it?"

Angelica, not looking at what she did, set down her wineglass on a fork, and it tipped over, spilling the rest of its contents onto the white tablecloth. The dark stain spread like a pool of blood. But none of us moved to pick up the glass.

"Close it," Angelica said, and there was a catch in her voice. "For how long?"

"For as long as it takes to get answers."

AFTER ANGELICA GOT HOME from the police station on Saturday afternoon, I called her to ask if I could bring food. It turned out that Carlo had already delivered enough food for twelve people, but she couldn't eat a bite. Gone was her usual cheerful tone of voice. She sounded so blue it broke my heart.

"How about I come over, and we watch *Cake Boss* on TV?" I said.

"I couldn't bear it." Her voice broke. "I have a headache. I'd better go lie down again."

The next morning, instead of asking whether I could come over, Nat and I showed up on her doorstep. We came with provisions. I carried a brown paper bag from Martini's Italian Market with egg-and-bacon sandwiches. Nat held plastic bowls of fruit salad and cups of freshly squeezed orange juice.

He craned his neck to study the facade of Angelica's house. "Not surprising that her home looks so nice."

Angelica's home was an older red-brick house with two floors. It was a modest one-family home, probably from the 1940s, and the rooms inside must be small and dark, certainly compared to what people expected from their houses today.

But it was quaint. White shutters contrasted nicely with the red brick, and trellises on either side of the entrance supported white climbing roses.

"Those roses look like fondant," Nat remarked. "In fact, the whole house looks like a cake."

We rang the doorbell, and a few moments later, the door opened.

Angelica wore a bathrobe. At the sight of us, her eyebrows shot up. "Bernie. Nat. What are you doing here?"

"You haven't had breakfast, have you?" I said. "I didn't think so. Let us in before the food gets cold."

Angelica stepped aside. I was deliberately being bossy—I didn't want her to make an excuse and send us away. She was always taking care of everyone else. This time, she'd have to let us mother her a bit.

Inside, to my surprise, the house was bright and airy. Walls had been knocked down, turning one half of the first floor into a single space on the left. The living and dining room merged with an open kitchen. To the right, a staircase led up to the second floor, presumably to the bedrooms.

Images of baked goods covered the walls. Photographs cozied up to water colors. Oil paintings nestled next to acrylics. Everywhere you looked, your eyes feasted on a dizzying array of cakes and cookies and other confectionary: cannoli, pignoli, amaretti, cuccidati, struffoli, anginetti, pizzelle, panettone, biscotti.

How could anyone live surrounded by these images and not be in a state of constant hunger?

Angelica led us to the kitchen. A counter ran along the walls in a long L, and a wide island sat in the middle, conveniently doubling as a breakfast bar and a workspace.

Silently, Angelica pulled the food from the bag and put the sandwiches on plates and the fruit in bowls and poured the juice into glasses. She arranged everything on the island. While she set the table, I found cups and turned on her espresso machine, making a *caffé lungo* for each of us.

Learning to make a caffé lungo had been one of my first lessons as a barista at Moroni's. When I'd come to Carmine, I had known how to make lattes and cappuccinos and Americanos, but I'd never come across a lungo. Basically, it was a single-serving espresso with enough water run through the filter for two shots, resulting in a kind of mini Americano. Since discovering it, I'd come to prefer it over the ubiquitous Americano—a lungo often retained more of the froth, the *crema*, and tasted more fully of the coffee bean.

Oh, Bernie, you've truly become a coffee snob.

I was all right with that. There was nothing like a damn fine cup of coffee.

I put the coffee cups on the island as Angelica indicated the stools.

"Go ahead, sit."

The three of us ate in silence for a while. I'd come charging into Angelica's home, like a bull in a china shop. Now the bull, without any real plan, had grown shy, wary of breaking the porcelain. I hoped Angelica needed us here. I hoped the companionable silence would help Angelica find her words.

So, I kept my mouth shut, except to bite into Martini's delicious bacon-and-egg sandwich.

Finally, Angelica did speak.

"He was not a good man," she said. "But he didn't deserve to die."

She took a sip of coffee. She put down the cup and stared at her plate, a frown on her face, as if she owed the half-eaten sandwich an apology.

"Am I a bad person?" she asked.

"A bad person?" Nat asked. He snorted, making clear what he thought of that idea.

"Not in a million years," I said. "What makes you say such a thing?"

"Because I feel as much grief for Moroni's as I do for Marty." She looked down at her lap. "Probably more."

"Well, that's a relief," Nat said. "So you are a human being, after all, not an angel from heaven above. I had my doubts, you know."

I nodded. "Angelica, the fact that you feel any grief for Marty is a sign that you're an exceptionally generous person. Didn't you yourself say that your biggest wish was to become friends with him again? A bad person wouldn't be so nice."

"Plus, Moroni's performs a public service," Nat said. "Without your cannolis, Carmine would fall into a deep depression."

I wasn't certain whether Nat meant a mental or economic depression. Maybe both.

"My cannolis." Angelica put a hand on her throat and let out a miserable groan. "How will Carlo manage without my cannolis? It's part of his lunch and dinner menus—his customers expect them."

Nat and I looked at each other. Was he thinking what I was thinking? So often he was.

Carlo's customers would survive without cannolis. But my worry was that if Angelica sat at home and worried about her brother's restaurant and her bakery, she was the one who'd fall into a deep depression. The cannolis, I'd just realized, were the answer.

"You're right," I told Angelica. "Carlo needs those cannolis. But with the bakery closed, what can we do?"

I waited a beat. Nat watched Angelica. We both did.

"Well," Angelica said. She surveyed the surrounding

kitchen, as if taking stock of what she saw. "My kitchen is compact, but I could easily make a few cannolis here."

"Enough for Carlo?"

"Maybe…"

Angelica usually got energized as soon as she had a project that could bring joy to others. But she didn't seem convinced. I had hoped she would immediately brighten at the idea, but her shoulders sagged, her eyes looked hollow. Perhaps she needed another nudge.

"What if you made cannolis, plus an unusual cake for Carlo's customers?" I suggested. "Something he could offer as a special dessert?"

She stared empty-eyed at her kitchen and then sighed.

"I guess I could make a *cassata*…"

"What's a cassata?"

"It's a layered cake with almond flour dough and a ricotta cream topping. At the end you decorate it with candied fruit, which makes it not just tasty but also pretty. I've got an old recipe from Sicily."

She slid off the stool, excusing herself. She shuffled past us. We could hear her heavy tread on the stairs. Then the creaking of the floor upstairs revealed she was in one of the bedrooms.

"Well done," Nat whispered to me.

"I'm not sure if it'll work. She's not her usual cheerful self, not without the bakery."

"Keeping her busy at home is better than nothing."

I hoped Nat was right. Because I had no other ideas for making her feel better.

A couple of minutes later, Angelica returned to the kitchen, a puzzled look on her face.

"I just can't find that notebook. You know, the one I told you about, Bernie—the one with the recipes I learned on my trip to Italy. When I couldn't find it at the bakery, I was sure I must have left it at home. But I've looked everywhere." Tears welled in her eyes. "Where could it have gone?"

"Don't worry, it'll turn up," Nat said, his head bent over his phone as he tapped and swiped. "Meanwhile, you can get started with this."

He held out his phone, showing us both a recipe for "Sicilian Cassata."

Angelica reluctantly agreed to rely on the online recipe, with a few modifications, and she began rummaging in the cupboards and drawers in the kitchen, pulling out bowls and spatulas and measuring cups.

"Oh, no." She pulled open more cupboards and drawers. Her voice cracked. "Oh, no..."

"What is it, Angelica?"

"I don't have any piping bags or cannoli forms at home. They're at the bakery."

She sat down on a stool, and it was as if all the air leaked out of her. Her whole body sagged, and she put her head in her hands.

"I can't..." Her voice sounded strained, on the verge of sobbing. "I can't make cannolis without my bags and forms..."

I gave Nat a helpless look. If Angelica broke, I would break, too. Carmine itself might break. Frantically, I thought of a solution. "We can buy new ones."

"None of the stores around here carry the right kind..."

"Can we borrow them from someone?"

Angelica shook her head.

I wouldn't give up so easily. If Angelica's own cannoli forms and piping bags would save the day, I would get them. Somehow.

An idea came to me.

"Right," I said, slipping off my stool. "The bakery might be a crime scene, but the cannoli forms and piping bags weren't used to murder anyone. They're harmless. I bet Chief Tedesco will let me pick them up for you."

"You really think so?" Angelica said. "You think she'll allow it?"

The child-like hope in her voice was heartbreaking. She was desperate for this to work.

"She'll allow it, all right."

I wanted to add, "If I have to kill her," but considering the circumstances, references to killing seemed in poor taste.

I pulled out my phone and dialed Chief Tedesco.

As the phone rang, I tapped my foot nervously.

This has got to work, Bernie. It has got to work.

NAT GAVE me a ride to Moroni's, dropping me off on his way to Martini's, where he would buy ingredients for Angelica— she needed about 90 ounces of ricotta.

I stood in front of Moroni's, my hands in my pockets. The black-and-yellow crime tape stretched across the entrance, and a warm breeze crinkled it. Beyond the glass in the door, the café was dark. Abandoned.

The break-in had been bad. This was so much worse.

A police cruiser pulled up to the curb. Chief Tedesco got out. So did Officer Fontana.

"This isn't exactly by the book," Chief Tedesco said, and slammed the door behind her. "But since the things you mentioned aren't part of the investigation, I'm fine with it."

Officer Fontana came around the car and greeted me with a nod.

Although I still had my keys, the police had Angelica's, and Chief Tedesco insisted that she and Fontana would remove the crime-scene tape and unlock the door.

Inside, the bakery looked the same as always. I'd expected a body-shaped outline on the floor, but of course Marty had been sitting in the chair when they found him.

I gave the area a wide berth, the image of Marty's dead body flashing across my mind again. I hurried through the back door. In the bakery, I found the cannoli forms and piping bags.

"Got everything," I said and turned around.

Chief Tedesco stood in the doorway, her arms crossed. She was staring at me.

"What?" I asked.

"Bernie." She glanced over her shoulder, apparently checking where Fontana was. She lowered her voice. "We need to talk."

The frown on her face told me this was serious.

"I visited Crystal Alfano, Marty's widow. She handed over Marty's computer. Angelica appears to have emailed Marty, inviting him to come to Angelica's."

I was shocked. "But it was Marty who invited himself over. Angelica got a note."

"Angelica mentioned the note yesterday." Chief Tedesco sighed. "But we have found no note."

"That's not possible. It's right in the office. Come see for yourself."

I led her into the little office.

Pins and needles prickled my spine. I looked down at the floor. I looked at the corkboard. It was empty. The note was gone.

"It was right here," I said. "Next to the hook for the extra set of keys."

I described the note, neatly folded and pinned to the board. I also recounted, as best I could remember, what Marty's note had said.

"That was the funny thing. He asked Angelica not to tell anyone, not even her closest friends and family."

"That is strange," Chief Tedesco said. "Why would it disappear? If Angelica killed Marty—"

"She didn't kill Marty," I snapped.

Chief Tedesco held up a hand to calm me. "All right, but if we're to *believe* she killed Marty, then she had no interest in destroying the note. It wouldn't benefit her. In fact, the note is evidence that supports her version of events." She looked thoughtful. "Anything else missing?"

I thought about that. "Well, maybe..."

The recipe book. Angelica had mentioned it a couple of times now. It seemed like the kind of thing that could easily go missing, and yet why would she misplace it?

I told Chief Tedesco, and she scratched the back of her neck. "The note from Marty and a notebook containing recipes..."

My heart skipped a beat. "Wait, without the note, it looks like Angelica was the one to set up the meeting. Which incriminates her. And the notebook contains the recipes for the cookies that killed Marty. If someone wanted to poison him and make it seem like Angelica did it, the notebook would be a big help."

"That's it, Bernie. Angelica made the cookies and left them in the café overnight. You ate one, so did Nat and Angelica. Obviously not poisoned. The killer would have had to bake the same cookies, adding poison to the batter. Then break into Moroni's and replace the safe batch. At the same time, they took the note from Marty, further incriminating Angelica."

"Only the note was never from Marty—it was a setup." I thought for a moment. "But what about the notebook? The killer must have taken that earlier. He or she needed time to bake the cookies."

"Right. Which means the killer had access to the bakery on at least two occasions—first to steal the notebook, and then to swap the cookies and take the note."

We looked at each other.

"The burglary," we said in unison.

"But there were only signs of forced entry the first time," Chief Tedesco said. "So how did the killer get into the bakery again?"

I stared at the corkboard.

Oh, no...

"Chief," Officer Fontana said, sticking his head through the door. "We've got a possible B and E in progress."

Chief Tedesco gave him a thumbs up and then turned to me. "Bernie, we need to lock up again."

I grabbed her arm, stopping her before she could step away.

"The hook," I said. "The extra set of keys used to hang on that hook. But I haven't seen them for days. In fact, I can't remember seeing them since the burglary."

"Which means—"

"Which means," I cut in, "that the killer broke into Moroni's, stole not only the notebook with the recipe for mustaccioli cookies but also the extra set of keys. The security camera is still broken. With the keys, the killer could easily get into the bakery, swap the cookies, and remove the note."

"Making it look like Angelica did it."

"Framing her."

Chief Tedesco nodded.

"I'm going to find this killer and—" I said.

"Whoa, whoa, Eve Silver, slow down." Chief Tedesco put a hand on my arm. "You've been a big help in the past, but you're not a detective, remember? This is my case to solve."

"But I—"

"You will stay out of the investigation." She raised her voice. "And that's my final word."

She leaned through the doorway, glancing down the hallway. Apparently satisfied Officer Fontana was gone, she whispered, "But if you do some quiet sleuthing, how will I know?"

She gave me a wink.

4

"Chief Tedesco wants you to snoop for her?" Nat sounded incredulous. "I swear, if this were the Old West, she'd have pinned a star on your chest and called you 'deputy.'"

The casual shrug I gave Nat didn't reflect how I'd felt earlier that day. The whole thing had amazed me. Who could have predicted that Chief Tedesco, who'd once tried to pin a murder on me, would trust my sleuthing abilities enough to want me as her unofficial eyes and ears on a case? But now that Chief Tedesco had accepted that I would "snoop," as Nat put it, I was eager to get started.

I would find this killer, clear Angelica's name, and make sure Moroni's opened for business again.

Nat and I were sitting at the bar at the Old Mill, drinking beers and talking through the events of the past few days. I loved the Old Mill almost as much as I loved Moroni's.

The Old Mill had once been a sawmill. Long after they had shut the mill down, the beautiful, old wooden building had been converted into a bar. A long hardwood counter dominated the room. Along the right-hand wall were booths, and near the entrance stood an old-fashioned jukebox. Chris Isaak was crooning from the speakers. A faint scent of pine resin perfumed the air.

The bartender, Jerry, moved behind the bar, restocking the bottles of booze neatly lined up on shelves in front of a mirror. He sported a big beard and a flannel shirt. He rarely spoke in more than a single syllable at a time, and had limited tonight's greeting to a nod.

"So, tell me again, who would have known Marty was coming to visit Angelica?" Nat asked.

"Well, no one. The killer must have set the whole thing up. The note was a hoax."

Nat looked thoughtful. "The killer knew what Marty's favorite cookie was."

"So?"

"Do you know what my favorite cookie is?"

I shook my head.

He grinned. "In case you ever plan to poison me, it's good old chocolate chip."

"Peanut butter," Jerry said. He stood a few feet from us, placing a bottle of bourbon on the shelf. "I like peanut butter cookies."

I couldn't find words to answer. It was possibly the longest sentence I'd ever heard Jerry speak. Nat's jaw had dropped. Clearly as surprised as I was.

"Uh," I said. "Good to know, Jerry."

Jerry's beard stretched into a smile. Then he got back to work, apparently satisfied with his contribution.

"What about you?" Nat asked me.

I took another slurp of beer and thought about it. "You know, I'm not sure whether I have a favorite cookie. It's like picking a favorite movie or song. Honestly, I can't. It totally depends on my mood. Am I in the mood to watch *Casablanca* or *Romancing the Stone* or *Moonstruck*? Do I feel like listening to Dean Martin or Madonna or Mozart? Do I have a craving for a pignoli or oatmeal or ginger snap cookie?"

"I can see you'll be hard to kill," Nat said. "But the point I'm trying to make is that Marty was hard to kill, too. Mustaccioli cookies aren't your run-of-the-mill choice."

He had a good point. Marty wasn't exactly Mr. Popular. I suspected there was a long list of people who disliked him. But the way he was killed—poisoned by his favorite dessert—suggested an intimate connection.

"So, who would be close enough to Marty to know what his favorite cookie was?"

"Crystal, most obviously," Nat said. "Angelica, too, of course. Maybe he has siblings or past lovers. I don't know. What about his dentist?"

"I don't think anyone dares tell their dentist about their cookie-eating preferences, or else they lie and say they eat sugar-free cookies."

Nat took a swig of beer. "I'll have to make a note of that for my next dentist appointment: 'Don't mention cookies.'"

That made a lightbulb blaze in my mind. There was another important clue to this closeness: the note.

"Listen, Angelica believed the note she received actually came from Marty. Which means the handwriting had to be convincing. The killer not only knew what Marty's favorite cookie was, they also knew his handwriting—at least well enough to fake it."

Nat thought about that for a moment. "Yeah, why didn't the killer send an email? Why drop off a note?"

"An email is hard to erase."

"Exactly. And easy to trace."

I set down my beer on the bar with a thunk.

"We need to look at that email," I said. "Maybe it'll reveal a clue. Crystal may have access to Marty's emails."

Nat gave me Crystal's contact information, and I sent her a message at once, asking if we could meet. Within seconds, I got a response.

> Meet me tomorrow afternoon at my parents' place. XO!

"XO? Remember how rude she used to be? Now she's sending me hugs and kisses."

Nat shrugged. "People change. Crystal has really transformed from mean girl to nice."

It was true. People did change. But sometimes they changed for the worse. At the garden party, Crystal, standing by Marty's side, had seemed miserable, and Angelica had recently told me that Crystal felt lonely—abandoned by her often-absent husband.

Nat stared at me. "Wait, you don't actually think Crystal could have killed Marty?"

I wasn't sure what I thought yet.

CRYSTAL'S PARENTS lived in a mansion down the street from Barry Longo's ostentatious house. Significantly, though, it sat on the corner of Cedar Hill Road, one foot firmly placed in the land of the rich.

The house had once been a Victorian, but a series of additions and extensions had transformed its character. Hardly any space was left for the lawn because of a long sunporch, and standing in the driveway and looking up at the upper stories, I got an instant crick in my neck. The synthetic slate roof had such a steep pitch that it seemed intent on taking flight. There was a widow's walk as well as a massive New Orleans-style, wrought-iron balcony, which contrasted poorly with a set of bay windows and a modernist porthole that looked like a massive monocle. The garage doors stood open, revealing a BMW and a Tesla within.

"Understated," Nat said.

The doorbell, when Nat pressed it, triggered a chiming inside that reminded me of a game show jingle. The kind of game show where people won millions.

The door opened. Crystal stood in the doorway, panting.

"I had to run to catch the door," she said. "But I can't, so I walked, and now I feel like I ran, anyway. I'm telling you, this pregnancy stuff is crazy. Walking is like running, except slower than crawling. Most of the day I'm sleepy, but at night I'm wide awake. And I've got gas, let me tell you—"

"Uh, Crystal," I interrupted, wanting to hear less about her intestinal woes. "Do you think we could come in?"

In the hallway, a massive chandelier dangled above our heads, glittering like diamonds. A staircase with a polished banister ran to a landing, which then led to more stairs leading upward. On the walls were paintings—original artwork, I guessed—including a few portraits. One of them, an oil painting, depicted a younger Crystal in a ball gown, half-smiling, half-sneering at the artist.

She showed us into a living room with a set of marshmallow-like armchairs and sofas, two of each.

"Beware of the armchairs." Crystal sat on a sofa. "They're so soft that once you sit, you can't get up again."

"Thanks for seeing us, and sorry to disturb you," I said, as I sank into an armchair. Next to me, Nat did the same, a look of surprise on his face as the soft cushions swallowed him.

Crystal waved my comment away. "Honestly, I'm happy you guys came. I'm going crazy here at my parents. They worry about me being alone, but then all they can talk about is their country club and tennis and golf. It's *sooo* boring." She sighed. "To be fair, though, I couldn't stand to stay another night in that big, lonely place in Short Hills. It's cozier here."

Cozier? I looked around and wondered about Crystal and Marty's home in Short Hills—was it the size of the White House? If so, I could understand why Crystal wasn't happy about staying there alone.

Maybe I should have felt envious of the giant mansions that she called home, but it wasn't for me: I was happy with my tiny ranch-style house on Lampedusa Lane. That was truly cozy.

I nudged the conversation toward the topic I wanted to discuss.

"I'm sorry for your loss."

Crystal snorted. "Big loss."

I sat up—or tried—and sank back down in my chair.

"You mean, you're not upset about Marty...?"

"Being killed? Sure. That part is awful. Anyone getting killed is awful. But I won't miss the bastard."

I glanced at Nat, who was struggling to sit up straight in the quagmire of the soft armchair. He returned my look, though. We hadn't expected Crystal to be so blunt.

"Oh, it was my own fault, of course," she went on. "I married Marty for his money. I wouldn't have admitted it at the time—I thought it was love—but really, I was attracted to his success and his bank account. But you know what? It turned out to be a horrible mistake."

"Why?"

"His money appealed to me, but his personality didn't. It was fine when we first met, and I was his shiny new trophy to put on display. But after a while, he showed his true colors. He was cruel and neglectful, especially after I got pregnant." She stroked her belly and smiled. "At least something good has come out of my time with Marty."

"How was he cruel?"

"He cheated on me. First, I believed he was on business trips all the time. Often it was true. He'd go to business dinners or events, and I'd ask if I could come. He said it wasn't appropriate to bring his pregnant wife. 'You'd be bored,' he told me. When I insisted I wouldn't, he said that he would. 'Pregnant women are no fun. You stay at home, where you belong.'"

"What a jerk," Nat said.

"But see, it wasn't only about me being boring. After a while, I suspected he went to the events on his own so that he could meet women. He'd go on all these 'overnight business trips,' and I became convinced he was staying at a hotel with someone else. So I confronted him. He called me 'paranoid' and 'irrational' and 'hysterical.' He said my hormones were making me crazy. For a while, I even believed him. Maybe he was right. Maybe I was nuts." A smile spread across her face. "But then I caught him."

"You caught him having an affair?"

"Yup. I saw text messages on his phone from a woman. Intimate stuff with plenty of emojis: pink hearts, rainbows, and unicorns, like she was some stupid kid. This time, when I confronted him with evidence, he confessed. He promised he would end it, and he'd devote himself entirely to me and the baby." She laughed, sounding cynical. "As if I believed him. He might have ended that affair, but eventually he'd cheat on me again."

"Who was the woman he had an affair with?"

"Who knows? Besides, I don't think she was the only one."

"So, did he take you to Barry Longo's party to show you he'd changed?"

"That's right. And I wasn't just bored, I was also frustrated. Marty would disappear now and then. I'm pretty sure he was sneaking off to flirt with women, even while I was there."

I had to ask a delicate and difficult question. Crystal had been blunt with us. I decided to reciprocate.

"Crystal, where were you the night before Marty was killed?"

"Sleeping at our home in Short Hills. Or trying to sleep, anyway."

"Could anyone corroborate that?"

"'Corroborate.'" Crystal laughed. "You sound just like Chief Tedesco. She asked me, too, of course. Marty was, for once, sleeping at home that night. So was Little Sprout here..." She tapped her belly. Then looked thoughtful. "Marty got a call in the middle of the night, but that was a wrong number, and otherwise no other human could confirm I was at home and in bed."

"No other human?"

"Yeah, we have security cameras. If anyone was paranoid, it was Marty. But my own parents are no different."

She pointed out a discretely placed camera, mounted in a corner of the ceiling.

"Chief Tedesco already looked into this. The security company pulled the feed, and the footage confirms that

Marty left early, but I didn't leave the house until late the next morning—after I got the call from the police."

I let out a long sigh. It surprised me how relieved I was that Crystal had a solid alibi. It wasn't long ago that I had disliked her. But then I'd learned that she was struggling with loneliness in a difficult marriage, and I'd come to sympathize. The ordeal had transformed her. She had actively wanted—and tried—to change, and she was a nicer person now.

Plus, there was another reason I was glad we could rule out Crystal.

"We need your help," I said.

"You do?"

She sounded genuinely surprised. I had the feeling Crystal rarely got called on to help anyone.

"We do," I confirmed. "Angelica is being framed for Marty's murder."

I explained how the evidence pointed to Angelica and why this had led to the bakery being closed. As I described the funk it had sent Angelica into, Crystal frowned.

"When I was most alone, Angelica turned out to be my only real friend. I'll do anything for her."

"So you'll help us find Marty's murderer?"

"For Angelica, yes. What do you need?"

I explained we needed to see the email from Angelica.

"The cops took Marty's laptop," Crystal said.

"Oh, right."

"But don't worry." She smiled. "I have his password written down at our home—my home—in Short Hills. I'll go right now and get it and log on via a browser, and then we can meet here tomorrow again."

There was determination in Crystal's voice, and she

clearly tried to underscore it by getting to her feet. But with her pregnant belly, she struggled to get off the sofa.

"Ugh. Why does this have to be so hard?"

I gave her a hand and pulled her out of the soft sofa.

"Uh," Nat said behind me, floundering in the armchair. "I think I need a hand, too."

5

Tuesday morning, I returned to Angelica's to help her make cannolis for Carlo's.

She was clearly keeping busy with baking projects. In fact, she'd made more cannolis and cakes for Carlo than she'd done when the bakery was open. She'd crammed every surface of her kitchen with Tupperware filled with cookies or cakes, leaving a few gaps in which to work. The coffee table in the living room was covered, too, as was her small, round dining table.

"You think there are enough cookies and cakes?" I asked her.

She surveyed her creations, a crease forming between her eyebrows.

"Maybe I should make more."

"Angelica, I was joking. Carlo's customers can't eat all these." I gestured at the dozens and dozens of containers. How much Tupperware could one person own, anyway? "Carlo will have to give them away."

"That's a good idea," Angelica said. "And you and Nat can eat the rest."

I smiled. "That was really what I was hoping you'd say."

Despite the crazy hoarding of cookie containers, maybe this baking therapy worked for her.

She grabbed a blob of dough and smacked it onto the countertop and dug her fingers into it, kneading and pounding it. The dough didn't stand a chance. She leaned into it, the muscles in her arms straining visibly, and she huffed. By the time she was steamrolling the dough with a rolling pin, beads of sweat sprung from her forehead.

I bit my lip, a new worry welling up. Had Angelica simply traded melancholy for mania? If she kept up this pace, she'd collapse.

An apron hung from a hook next to the fridge. I grabbed it and put it on.

"All right, let me help," I said, rolling up my sleeves. "Let's make some cookies."

We powered through half a dozen recipes at the same time: lemon and pignoli and plain almond-paste cookies, followed by pizzelle, amaretti, and torcetti. And, of course, more cannolis for Carlo's dessert menu.

Halfway through the morning, my hands and back ached, but Angelica showed no signs of slowing down.

I'd promised to walk the latest batch of cannolis over to Carlo's on my way to meet Nat for lunch at the Old Mill— after which we'd go to Crystal's again. But I hesitated to take the apron off. Could I leave Angelica on her own in the state she was in?

Maybe I should stay...

I looked around, taking stock of the half dozen trays of prepped cookies that stood balanced on chairs and on top of the fridge, and I realized that my help had only increased productivity, not reduced Angelica's frenzy.

Only one thing will calm her...

I needed to make progress on the investigation, find the killer, and reopen Moroni's. I undid the apron and took it off. Angelica barely looked up when I said goodbye.

"Don't forget the cannolis," she said as she pressed cookie shapes into the flattened dough.

I headed out into the sunshine, carrying a big tray of Saran-wrapped cannolis.

The sun was warm. The air was fresh. I stood on the sidewalk for a moment, closing my eyes and breathing deeply.

I felt guilty for leaving Angelica, and even more guilty for being so relieved to escape. But what good was I in the kitchen? My best chance was to catch Marty's killer, restore Moroni's to its usual perfection, and make Angelica smile again.

The walk into town took me about 20 minutes. I was careful not to trip over a tree root or a crack in the sidewalk. By the time I got to Garibaldi Avenue, I had prayed to Saint Honoré, the patron saint of bakers, seven times, hoping he would want the cannolis to survive the trip as much as I did.

I turned onto Carmine's main street and stopped.

A man was standing by Moroni's, half a block from me. He leaned close to the window, a hand shading his eyes as he peered into the bakery.

I walked toward him.

"Excuse me," I said, intending to explain why the bakery was closed.

He whipped around, and then took a couple of steps backward, clearly startled.

His appearance was as strange as his behavior. He wore a floppy hat, like the kind fishermen wear, pulled down his forehead. A large pair of sunglasses covered his eyes. As if those two accessories weren't enough to cover his face, he wore a trench coat with the collar turned up, despite the balmy day.

"You're wondering about the bakery—" I began.

"No, no," he muttered in a gruff voice. "No interest."

His voice sounded unnatural, like he was putting on an act. I'd been around enough bad actors to know.

He backed away some more. His disguise swaddled him, and it was impossible to tell who he really was. I cocked my head and peered at him. And yet—he looked vaguely familiar.

"Do I know you?"

He tensed. "No, I'm sure you don't."

"Look, mister—"

But I didn't have time to finish my sentence. He turned on his heels and scurried off, hurrying across the street, dodging a van, and yanking open the door to a parked car.

His behavior raised my suspicion. Why was he snooping around Moroni's? What if he had something to do with the murder? Didn't killers often return to the scene of the crime, drawn back by compulsion or a desire to gloat?

If I moved fast, I could catch up with him, I could—

I lunged forward, forgetting the burden I held in my hands. I tripped. The tray slipped from my grasp. Disaster slowed time to a crawl. The cannolis wiggled free from the baking paper and slid out from under their blanket of Saran wrap.

"Oh, no—"

A cannoli exploded on the sidewalk. Then another. A third victim splattered the concrete as I fumbled for control of the tray.

I gripped the edges firmly, raising it. They stopped sliding. They were safe.

My heart was pounding. I exhaled. Three cannolis lay

broken on the sidewalk, the victims of my overeager clumsiness.

Stuppiad.

I should have let the cannolis crash. Every single one, if necessary. A few desserts coming to a sticky end didn't matter much. Angelica had made more than enough to replace them.

But as I stood on the sidewalk, clutching my baker's tray, the stranger's car revved and drove off. In the distance, it turned off Garibaldi Avenue, disappearing.

Had I saved the cannolis, but allowed Marty's killer to escape?

"You didn't get a good look at him? And what about his license plate?" Nat asked.

I shook my head.

Nat rested his jaw on his hand, elbow on the table, as he thought. "Well, he might simply have been a curious passerby, someone wondering why Moroni's was closed."

"Or he might have been the killer," I said.

Few people had come to the Old Mill for lunch today, and Nat and I sat in one of the coveted booths.

The Old Mill didn't serve meals, only drinks, but you were welcome to bring takeout. Our food was laid out on the table: Martini's famous Italian subs, lying on their butcher paper like unpacked Christmas presents. We were both drinking Cokes with lots of ice.

While we ate, savoring the salami, provolone, and roasted peppers that made Martini's subs special, not to mention the dressing, we talked about our conversation with Crystal the day before.

"You know, I admire her honesty," I said. "I feel she's come a long way in becoming more honest with herself, too."

"All this appreciation and talk about feelings, Bernie—you should be a talk show host."

I stuck out my tongue at him, and he laughed.

Voices rose from a nearby booth, and it must have reminded Nat that we'd better keep our voices down. "But seriously," he said, leaning forward and speaking more softly. "If Crystal felt so strongly about Marty, I bet other people did, too. Which might make the list of suspects very long."

"True. But remember that the killer had to have access to the bakery the night it was burglarized and then the night before Marty died. That's got to narrow things down a bit."

"Listen, do you think—"

But Nat was interrupted by a man from the nearby booth, yelling. "There's a rat infestation, and the people of Carmine deserve to know."

Nat and I looked at each other. I recognized the voice. Nat did, too.

"Peter Piatek," he said.

Nat and I both leaned out of the booth to see what was happening. The young, self-made journalist and publisher of *The Carmine Enquirer*—the town's online newspaper—rose from a booth close to the restrooms at the back. His companion stood now, too.

"Calm down, Peter. Let's talk this through."

The other person was Dan Russo of Russo's Realty.

"I'm done talking, Dan. It's time to get writing."

Peter strode away from Dan, passing our booth. But when he saw us, he stopped.

"Hey, any news on the Alfano murder?" he asked.

He shifted from foot to foot, and even as he waited for our answer, he checked his wristwatch. I'd never seen him so harried.

"What makes you think we know anything?" I asked.

"Oh, come off it, Bernie. You're always sticking your nose into murders. By now, you probably know as much—or maybe more—than Chief Tedesco."

I mumbled something about not being a detective and just minding my own business.

Peter cut me off. "I don't have time for this. Bernie, when you're ready to talk, you know where my office is."

"Above Milano Books."

"Right."

He strode off. The front door to the Old Mill swung shut behind him.

Dan Russo leaned against the side of our booth, his arms crossed.

He sighed. "That kid sure can be a pain in the *culo*."

"*Culo* is Italian," Nat explained to me. "It means—"

"I know what it means, thanks. What was this about rats?"

"Well, sadly, Peter's right," Dan said. "There seems to be a problem with rats in Puccini Park. The real issue is that Mayor Blink denies it's true and refuses to do anything about it. I've been trying to convince him to take it seriously, since a rat infestation is no joke. Imagine what it could do to property values in Carmine?"

For Dan, falling property prices was a waking nightmare.

He shook his head sadly. "And it's not just property values in the long term. We've got the Italian Day Celebration coming up. That will take place in the park. Imagine if word gets out ahead of the event that we have an infestation

—or worse, rats swarm the party..." He grimaced, clearly imagining the worst. "So I asked Peter to hold off on the story until I could talk Mayor Blink into doing something. But Peter insists on running it. Readership of *The Carmine Enquirer* has dipped, and he says he needs another big break."

"I guess a murder case isn't enough," I said. "I have the feeling Peter's getting greedy for scoops."

As we talked to Dan, the front door to the Old Mill opened. Glancing that way, I saw a stranger approach the bar. He was tanned and had highlights in his hair, which made it look unnaturally sun streaked. He wore jeans and a light-blue button-down shirt. Setting down a laptop bag on the counter, he hailed Jerry and asked for mineral water with a "twist of lime."

"Who's that?" I asked. "He looks sort of familiar."

"He does look familiar," Dan said, frowning. Then his face brightened. "Oh, I know. He looks like Marty. It's got to be his brother."

It was true. The man bore a striking resemblance to the dead man—if Marty had been skinnier and graced with a full head of hair.

"I heard from Joanna that he was coming to town," Dan said. "Excuse me, I'd better say hello."

Dan headed to the bar. From where I sat in the booth, I watched him introduce himself and shake the man's hand. After a couple of minutes, though, Dan said goodbye and headed out, no doubt needing to get back to work. Marty's brother drank his mineral water and scrolled on his phone.

"I'll get refills," I told Nat.

He smirked at me, nodding at our half-full glasses. "Go ahead, Eve Silver."

I grabbed our glasses and headed to the bar, eager to talk to the new arrival.

At the bar, as Jerry refilled the glasses with Coke, I turned to Marty's brother.

I tried to sound casual. "Hi, there. Are you visiting Carmine? On business?"

"Funeral."

He kept looking at his phone. His curt answer and lack of eye contact were no doubt meant to put me off. But I persisted.

"Oh, that's terrible. I'm so sorry for your loss." I paused. "This isn't Marty Alfano's funeral you're going to, is it?"

The man glanced at me. He frowned. Then went back to his phone.

"Yes, it is."

"What a tragedy. And now the police are investigating..."

"The police know who did it."

"Oh?"

Finally, he looked up. "Yes, that awful woman. Marty's ex-wife, Angelica. She poisoned him."

I clenched my fists, resisting my desire to yell at him for calling Angelica "awful."

"I saw the local news coverage, and I can read between the lines. It's the oldest story in the world. Washed-up ex-wife murders successful businessman because she can't face the facts: she's old and single and won't ever snag a guy like that again."

I gripped the edge of the bar to keep from pummeling Marty's brother.

Jerry put down two fresh Cokes on ice. He looked down at my white-knuckled hand on the bar and raised an eyebrow. I let go. I grabbed the drinks. But as I was preparing to head back to Nat, I caught Marty's brother staring at me.

"Wait," he said. "I know you. You're that actress."

I sighed. "From *Silver & Gold*, yes."

"Yeah, Bernadette Kovac." He grimaced, as if my name tasted bitter. "You testified against Jay Casanova. I met Jay. Even went to some of his parties. He's a good guy."

"A good guy?" I said, incredulously.

After the trial, millions of Americans refused to believe that their beloved heartthrob, Jay Casanova, could be guilty of trafficking drugs. I got used to people hating me. I received death threats, including from Jay's own brother, Harry. Which was why I'd gone into witness protection. But Harry had been busted, and when he confessed and confirmed my testimony, Jay Casanova's popularity finally imploded. Except for a paparazzi who'd recently hounded me, few clung to the conspiracy theory that he'd been framed.

Could this guy really still believe that Jay was innocent?

"Jay was convicted," I said. "He was caught red-handed, and the jury agreed."

"So what? We all have our vices. The whole thing was a witch hunt. Your testimony was baloney. The jury was a bunch of puritans. The fact is that Jay should never have gone to prison. Maybe paid a fine or done some community service nonsense, so he could get back to making great movies and throwing the best parties in Los Angeles."

I bit my tongue. If I got mad, I'd lose my chance to learn more about Marty's brother.

"That's where you're from, Los Angeles?" I asked, forcing my voice to sound bright and friendly instead of furious.

He nodded. "I'm Rick Alfano, Marty's brother. You might

have heard of my company, HerbaTroo—America's fastest-growing online store for homeopathic remedies."

He patted his laptop bag, which had a logo stitched on it: a purple flower with the name *HerbaTroo* at its center.

"Never heard of it."

He leaned toward me.

"Can I let you in on a secret?"

Excitement fluttered in my stomach. A secret? Did he want to share an important clue about why Marty died?

"Yes, what?"

He smiled and leaned back on his barstool, reviewing me, as if I were an object to be studied. "You'd look a heck of a lot better if you lost 20 pounds. My herbal supplements wouldn't just tighten up those love handles. They'd also give your hair some much-needed shine. No man likes dull, lifeless hair on a woman. Do yourself a favor, sweetie, and look up HerbaTroo."

I gaped at him in astonishment. Did this guy believe the garbage that came out of his own mouth?

6

"Don't get me started on Rick Alfano."

Crystal had chosen the dining table for our meeting that afternoon, a welcome change from the quicksand couches. She had brought a laptop and was tapping at the keys, logging into Marty's account as she talked. Nat and I sat on either side of her as we told her about our encounter with Rick at the Old Mill.

"You know Rick well?" I asked her.

"I don't know him at all. The two brothers had been estranged for years. Marty wouldn't even mention Rick's name, and the couple of times I asked about his brother, he blew his top. Rick probably felt the same way. He didn't even come to our wedding. The first time I met him was yesterday. He was all smiles and condolences until he made some pretty unsubtle hints about the will. I told him Marty's wishes were clear: our baby and I get it all."

"How did he react to that?"

Crystal snorted. "Not well. He's got a temper. He started yelling about his rights and how he'd stood by his brother during his hardest years and blah, blah, blah. Then he stormed out."

Nat and I exchanged a look. No doubt Nat was thinking what I was thinking. Where there was money, there was a motive for murder. Though, of course, Rick lived in L.A. He wouldn't have been anywhere near Carmine when the break-in or the murder happened.

"Bingo," Crystal said. "I'm logged into Marty's account."

She clicked around. Marty used a single online service for email and file storage. This meant that, despite the police having the laptop, we could access everything via a web browser.

"Can you find the email from Angelica inviting Marty to the bakery?"

"Sure," Crystal said, and tapped away. "There it is."

I read the email. I'd seen messages from Angelica before. She used words like "wonderful" and "delighted" and "joy," punctuated by emoticons of hearts and laughing cats. This one was brief and uncharacteristically straightforward:

Dear Marty,

It was a pleasure to see you at the party. I need to discuss something extremely important with you related to money. You may profit from it. Not something to discuss on the phone.

Please come to the bakery tomorrow morning at 6:30 am. I'll make mustaccioli for you. And don't tell anyone you're coming. I need to keep this a secret. You'll understand.

Sincerely, Angelica.

"That doesn't sound like Angelica at all," Nat said.

"I agree. But the email says it's from 'Moroni's Italian Bakery.'"

"Maybe it's a fake."

I double-checked the email address, but it was the right email address.

"If it's the real email address," Crystal said, sounding thoughtful, "the killer probably hacked Angelica's account."

"Good point," I said. "And after breaking into her account—"

I stopped myself. "Breaking in." The words had set off a little explosion in my brain, synapse fireworks flaring and popping. I was waiting for the spectacle to die down, so I could make sense of what my mind was telling me.

"Maybe the killer didn't need to hack Angelica's account..."

Nat looked at me. "Then how—?" His eyes widened. "The break-in. You mean the killer broke into the bakery and used Angelica's computer to send the message?"

"Yes, but not during the original break-in. Look at when Marty received this message." I pointed to the date and time. "Around midnight the night before he was killed. I guarantee you that Angelica wasn't sitting at her laptop, emailing people at midnight. That confirms what we suspected: the killer went back to Moroni's that night, not only to swap Angelica's cookies for the poisoned ones, but also to send this email."

"Angelica doesn't have a password on her computer?" Nat asked.

"She does," I said, blushing on Angelica's behalf. "It's 1, 2, 3, 4."

Nat slapped his forehead. "Doh."

"Hey, don't knock it—that's my password, too," Crystal said.

Nat leaned back in his chair, looking thoughtful. "All

right, but what if Marty hadn't seen the email in time and got up late the next morning? The killer ran a big risk."

Crystal gasped. "I just remembered something. The night before Marty died, he got a phone call in the middle of the night. I was asleep, but it woke me up. He said it must have been a wrong number. But he sat on the edge of the bed and looked at his phone for a while, scrolling through messages. I bet after the call, he got distracted by his notifications. He always did. Every other minute, Marty was looking at his phone."

After thinking it through, I could see how the killer, no doubt knowing Marty's behavior around his phone, must have made the call to wake him, so he'd have time to see the email and leave early in the morning.

I relayed my theory to Nat and Crystal, and they agreed.

"If his favorite cookies didn't convince him," Crystal said, "I think the mention of money would. Marty only cared for two things: women and money."

"Which reminds me," I said, "how was he doing financially?"

"Good, but..."

"But what?"

Crystal shrugged. "No big thing. But I looked at our checking account, and it's flush. There is something unusual, though. Marty transferred large sums every third month. Over the past six months, he'd made no transfers."

"Have you looked through his files?" I asked, pointing at the screen.

"Not yet. Let's take a look."

Crystal double-clicked on the folders. Fortunately, they were well labeled and organized. Marty had a folder called "Banking," another "Real Estate," and a third "Investments."

"Let's start with banking and work our way through them all," I said.

"I'd better make some tea and coffee," Crystal said. "This could take a while."

Ten minutes later, she had served ginger-lemon herbal tea for herself and coffee for us, and we dove into the folders. Crystal scrolled through the spreadsheets and statements, and we discussed the details, helping each other see the big picture. None of us was a financial whizz. It took us time to make sense of the many spreadsheets and statements, even though they were in order.

Soon, I began to get a sense of Marty's finances. He had multiple investment accounts with different financial advisers—apparently he didn't believe in putting all your eggs into one basket. The bank statements confirmed what Crystal had said. Like clockwork, Marty always transferred sizable sums once a quarter. The sums varied in size, but they were usually above 100,000 dollars.

"It looks like he made a killing on real estate," I said, "and much of the profit went back into his stock market investments. Let's look at the 'Investments' folder."

We read more statements. It was dizzying to see the massive amounts of money that Marty had invested—in one day, he'd gambled more than I'd ever earned, and come away with a big profit. In fact, looking at his statements over time, a pattern emerged of Marty getting back more than he put in. But there were cracks in the pattern.

A spreadsheet summarized his profits and losses.

"What's this? It looks like his earnings begin to dwindle."

"That fits with when he began to transfer less money," Crystal said. "But what happened?"

"Maybe he got unlucky," Nat said.

"Maybe," I said, feeling there must be more to it than

that. "Open that statement. And then that one. And that one. Notice something?"

Crystal and Nat stared at the screen. I pointed out the spreadsheet summarizing the earnings and losses in the statements.

"Overall, it looks like he's making money throughout the year," Crystal said. "Nothing is marked 'loss.'"

"But wait," Nat said. "Then why is the bottom-line decreasing? Oh, I see. Look at the statements. It's because of all those transfers. They're not losses. They're marked 'reinvestment.'"

"Small transfers," Crystal said. "Lots of them."

"Yeah, they're small relative to the huge amounts Marty dealt with. But look at how much they amount to. Marty's made the calculation here. It's about 300,000 dollars. And these 'reinvestments' seemed to increase recently."

Crystal opened a series of PDF files. "If they're reinvestments, they'll be noted in these financial manager statements. And he also has an overview of his investment portfolio."

As she scrolled through the documents, I noted the numbers. Only one set of investment statements showed a consistent pattern of reinvestments, all tied to the same account.

"Looks like Marty noted all the sums that were supposed to be reinvested, and he added a comment. What does it say?"

Crystal clicked on the comment, and a little box popped up. "'Missing: reinvestment does not correspond with investment portfolio,'" she read. "What does that mean?"

"Wait a sec," Nat said. "If the financial manager reinvested the money, but Marty didn't see a corresponding investment in his portfolio, then where did the money go?"

"I bet that was Marty's question," I said. "Who is the financial manager for this account?"

Crystal scrolled to the top, so we could see whose name was listed in the header.

"Well, isn't that a funny coincidence?" Nat said.

I nodded. "Barry Longo."

7

"So, you'd like some investment advice?"

Barry Longo, smiling, poured coffee into our cups.

It was Wednesday morning, another sunny day, and I sat in a wicker chair at a wrought-iron table on his back patio. Glancing upward, I could see the bathroom window I had leaned out to eavesdrop on Marty and whoever he'd been talking to at the party.

"I'm coming into an inheritance," I said, repeating the story I'd told Barry on the phone to make my visit more plausible. "See, I heard about you from a friend. She invited me to your garden party."

"I remember you from the party," he said. "Who's your friend?"

"Crystal Alfano."

He shook his head, looking sad. "So sad about Marty. So sad."

"So sad," I agreed. I took a sip of coffee. "All this started before he died. I mentioned to Crystal that I needed investment advice, and she mentioned it to Marty, and he recommended you."

"He did?" Barry faltered, then recovered quickly. "Of course he did. Naturally, he would. We'd worked together for years."

"He did well investing with you."

"He did extremely well," Barry said, leaning back and weaving his fingers over his belly. He looked like a self-satisfied cat. Today, he wore a lime green polo shirt with a pair of yellow chinos. "All my clients have done extremely well. That's why they keep coming back."

"I'm glad to hear that, because I'm clueless about numbers and investing…"

Barry's Cheshire cat smile broadened. "That's why you came to me."

"I want to make sure this is a good long-term investment."

"Always. You can trust me to do what's best for you."

I paused and shifted in my seat. I crossed my legs. Then uncrossed them. In his eyes, I hoped I looked uncomfortable.

"The thing is, Marty told me—well, how do I put this without sounding rude?—that he'd had problems with your investments. Specifically reinvestments."

Did his smile falter a little? Was that a twitch in his left eye? He broke his joined hands and instead folded his arms across his chest.

"Problems?"

I nodded. "Losses."

He was silent for a moment. If he'd been stealing from Marty, as I suspected, I'd come awfully close to accusing him.

"Marty hit the jackpot with me," Barry said with a sigh.

"But the man was a risk-taker. He liked to go big. He wanted profit here and now, and if you're not willing to wait for slow, steady returns, then you're assuming a greater risk. You're more likely to lose some money."

"So he did lose money."

"Some. But he made more than he lost. I don't like to speak ill of the dead. But the thing about Marty was that he was quick to blame others, even if he himself had knowingly and willingly reinvested his profits in high-risk stocks."

"You're so right," I said quickly. "In Marty's mind, he was never to blame. Which is why I didn't take it seriously. If I had, I wouldn't be here, would I? Besides, Marty told me he was going to see you to straighten everything out anyway. And I guess you guys did."

This was a stretch, but I hoped Barry still bought my story because I needed to find out whether he'd talked to Marty about the losses. It would have given Barry a motive to murder Marty, after all—to cover up the theft.

Barry frowned. "Well, I can assure you, Marty never complained to me."

"That's strange. I was sure he mentioned it. In fact, he said he'd talked to you at the garden party." I frowned, trying to look uncertain. "Or was it that he was going to talk to you about setting up a meeting for Friday? I can't remember."

"It's possible Marty mentioned it at the party. I don't remember. But we wouldn't have met on Friday. I had the day off. In fact, I was out of town for the weekend, enjoying a visit to New York City." Barry's focus shifted to the coffee. "Another cup?"

He busied himself with refilling our cups.

"You must have plenty of clients in New York," I said, accepting the refill.

"I do. But this was a visit for pleasure, not business. My sister's birthday. I took her to a Broadway show and dinner, and then the next day, we went to Central Park and the Metropolitan Museum." He shook his head sadly. "What a shock to return, after a lovely weekend away, to the news of Marty's death."

I shook my head sadly, too, appearing to agree with his sentiment.

Then he sat up and smiled again. "But let's not dwell on sad things. Let's talk about how we can make you richer, eh?"

I returned the smile. "Yes, please."

Barry's laptop lay on the table. He opened it and ran through a slideshow that presented me with three investment options. Soon I was neck deep in a sea of "accruing interest" and "dividends" and other stock market lingo that threatened to drown me.

My mind drifted to the case.

Marty might have found out that Barry was stealing money and confronted him about it. That would explain why Marty had referred to the police at the garden party—he'd been snidely reminding Barry that he knew about his illegal activities. But Barry seemed to have an alibi. If he was in New York City, he couldn't have broken into Moroni's and swapped the cookies.

I asked Barry a few questions about the investment options, then promised I'd look over the details at home and get back to him as soon as possible. He promised to email me the presentation.

"Call me anytime," he said. "I'm happy to answer your questions."

We stood and shook hands, and I said I'd see myself out.

At the end of the patio, I headed around the corner of

the house. Glancing over my shoulder, I saw Barry was watching me.

Then I was around the corner, out of sight, and I stopped.

Barry was up to no good. I had done my best to seem convincing, but if he were clever, he would see through my act. A little eavesdropping might reveal how he'd react.

I pressed myself against the wall of the house, close to the corner, listening.

"Hey, buddy," I heard him say from the patio around the corner.

I stiffened, my heart thumping. His voice was so loud and clear that, for a second, I thought he was right next to me.

"Can you talk?" he said. "Listen, we've got to be careful. That Bernie woman was here with a story about wanting investment advice. She's obviously snooping around..."

Then a sliding door swished open and snapped shut, cutting off his voice.

BARRY LONGO'S FRONT YARD, no longer crammed with food stands and a massive sound system, seemed to have grown to twice its size. Free to dominate the space, the huge shady sycamore and the flowerbeds with their fall blooms were even more striking. I pulled open the wrought-iron gate to the street, and as I glanced back, I glimpsed Barry at a second-floor window. Then he was gone.

I wandered down the street, past Phil Palladino's neighboring home. It was twice the size of mine, but nowhere near the ostentation of Barry Longo's big box. Phil's garden had a coziness that suggested he handled it himself. In contrast, Barry probably paid a gardener to take care of everything. How much did it cost to maintain a property like this? Plenty, no doubt.

If Barry was such a successful investment guy, why did he need to steal from his clients? The answer was obvious: greed. Judging by his home and his lavish parties, Barry wanted to live like the super rich. If he couldn't afford to—like so many of us couldn't—maybe he was willing to break the law to get what he wanted.

There was no doubt that Barry was dabbling in crime.

Money was the root of all evil—or the lack of money was the root of all evil, according to Mark Twain—but did that mean that Barry had killed Marty? Not if he had an airtight alibi. I'd have to find out if his sister could corroborate it. Was that who he'd called? I doubted it. He'd referred to the person as "buddy" and to me as "that Bernie woman." Something about the words and tone of his speech suggested he'd been talking to a man.

The engine of a vehicle rumbled to life nearby. My mind was on Barry and who he might have called, so it took me a moment to register that a truck was pulling away from the opposite curb.

It was a mail truck. The driver flashed past me.

"Hey!" I called out.

The mail truck sped up. Who knew USPS mail trucks could drive so fast? It swung hard into a turn and its engine roared.

I broke into a run.

I sprinted down the sidewalk, dodging a dog walker, leaping around a tree. Hurtling around the corner, I caught the taillights flashing one last time in the distance before the truck turned again. I dashed up the street, but the truck was gone. By now, it would be blocks away. I'd never catch it.

I stopped, bending over and resting my hands on my knees, breathing hard.

Surely, no ordinary USPS truck could drive that fast.

Plus, through the window on the driver's side, I'd glimpsed the driver—and I could have sworn it was U.S. Marshall Roberta LaRosa.

8

"I've got good news," Chief Tedesco said. "The lab results confirmed the poison in the cookies—and we found more in the cocoa jar."

At that very moment, I was chomping down on a pignoli cookie and stopped. "That's good news?"

We'd congregated in Angelica's kitchen. I was sitting on a stool and so was Nat. Angelica craned over a bowl on the counter, energetically mixing batter, while Chief Tedesco leaned against the kitchen island, sipping a cup of coffee.

The police chief had shown up for lunch to provide an update on the investigation. Thanks to Martini's mortadella sandwiches, we were all well-fed, and now we were enjoying coffee and cookies.

Except Angelica. She kept herself busy baking, pouring her anxiety into the flour, butter, and sugar.

"It is good news," Chief Tedesco insisted. "Because the cocoa jar only had Angelica's fingerprints on it."

"You're going to have to help me out here," I told her. "That doesn't sound like good news."

"Angelica's fingerprints were smudged with traces of

cocoa powder. None of it contained the poisonous substance, aconitine, which suggests that either she put on gloves to add the poison or else—"

"—or else someone else did!"

"That's right. And it is good news because it helps me build my case that Angelica didn't kill Marty."

Angelica let out a long sigh. "Thank goodness..." She turned around, wiping her hands on her apron. "So you believe me?"

Chief Tedesco put down her cup with a thunk. "Of course I believe you," she said, sounding offended. "Why wouldn't I?"

"Well, it's only..."

I came to Angelica's aid. "It's only that another murder happened at a café in Carmine. And you were pretty convinced that I did the dirty deed."

"*Madone*," Chief Tedesco said, slapping her forehead. "I'll never forgive myself for being such a *stunad*. You were obviously innocent, and I should have seen it."

"That's all history."

She smiled at me. "Thanks, Bernie." She turned to Angelica. "And these lab results are really great news because I can safely conclude that the crime scene no longer needs to be secured."

"What—" Angelica put a hand on her chest, barely suppressing her emotion. "—what are you saying?"

"I'm saying you can reopen Moroni's tomorrow."

Angelica broke into a big smile. Nat and I jumped off our seats and gave Angelica a hug, then turned and gave Chief Tedesco a hug, too, which she accepted with awkward stiffness.

Nat and I stomped our feet and cheered. We should have been drinking champagne instead of coffee.

When I said so, Angelica shook her head. "Prosecco, *mia cara*. Let the French have their champagne. And anyway, I've got baking to do—let's save the bubbly for later."

Chief Tedesco put an arm around my shoulders and whispered in my ear. "Once I'm off duty, I won't say no to some Prosecco at the Old Mill."

"It's a date," I said.

It was impossible for me to even imagine any animosity between us. Chief Tedesco had gone from being my number one enemy to becoming a friend—someone I respected and genuinely liked. Life was full of wonderful surprises.

We got back to talking about the case. I settled onto my stool again. In between sips of coffee, I recounted my visit to Barry Longo's and how I believed that if Marty confronted Barry about stealing, we might have a motive for murder.

"You're right about his alibi, though," Chief Tedesco said. "He was in New York City the weekend of Marty's death. His sister, who says she was with him the whole time, confirmed it."

"Anyway," Nat added, "how likely is it that Marty's financial adviser knew about his obsession with a certain cookie?"

"Good point," I said.

The conversation reminded me of seeing Roberta LaRosa outside Barry Longo's home. I ought to tell Chief Tedesco, but somehow it felt like tattling on Roberta. Instead, I should try to track her down and find out what she was up to. Then, with her permission, I could tell the others.

I focused my thoughts on the case again.

"What was the poison in the cookies? Don't tell me it was arsenic."

"Ground aconitine," Chief Tedesco said. "The scientific

name is *aconitum napellus.* It's derived from a plant called monkshood or wolfsbane. The powder we found was in such a high concentration, a whiff of it would have killed an ox."

"How do you get hold of wolfsbane?"

Nat laughed. "Where do you get hold of anything? The internet."

He pulled out his phone and began searching. After a while, he looked up. "You can buy wolfsbane seeds and grow the plant yourself. Looks like it's not just deadly, but also pretty—the purple flowers are, anyway. But I'm not sure how easy it is to find ground aconitine. It turns up in small quantities in a lot of other stuff, though. There are even herbal medicines that say they contain *aconitum napellus.* My search turned up a few homeopathic medicines."

My gut tightened into a fist. I reached for Nat's phone and yanked it out of his hands.

"Hey, Bernie, what's up...?"

I ignored his look of surprise. If I turned out to be right...

I scrolled through the search results, moving my thumb fast. As Nat had said, you could buy wolfsbane seeds. Plus, there were plenty of websites describing the toxicity of aconitine. I scrolled past a couple of sites advertising home-opathic remedies, and I was beginning to think my hunch had been wrong.

Then I hit the bullseye.

"I knew it."

I turned the phone for the others to see. Nat, Chief Tedesco, and Angelica crowded around the little screen.

"What are we looking at?" Nat asked. "A homeopathic treatment for chronic headache? Oh, it contains *aconitum napellus.*"

"Right," I said. "Now look at the name of the company."

Nat's eyes widened. "HerbaTroo—that's Rick Alfano's company."

There was a shocked silence.

Then Nat said, "But he's from Los Angeles. He only showed up after Marty's death."

"Not quite true," Chief Tedesco said. "Rick has admitted to being on business in the TriState area for the past two weeks. He's been staying in New York City."

"*Mamma mia*," Angelica said. "So he could have driven to Carmine..."

I nodded. "The guy's got motive, means, and opportunity. He could be our killer."

THE NEXT DAY felt like Christmas.

Except the sun was shining down on Garibaldi Avenue, casting long morning shadows. Chief Tedesco removed the crime scene tape, and it was as if she were unwrapping Moroni's.

She turned and handed Angelica the keys. "It's all yours."

Angelica beamed, hugging the keys to her chest. Her eyes glistened.

"Come on," I said. "Open up. I need a cup of coffee."

I'd been too excited this morning to grab coffee at home. Long before my alarm was set to go off, I'd leaped out of bed, streaked through the shower, and wrestled into clothes, only realizing as I hurried down the street how horribly mismatched everything was: black jeans with a baby blue t-shirt clashing with a pair of cranberry sneakers. Whatever. I had to get to Moroni's in time to join Angelica and Chief Tedesco.

Now that Angelica was unlocking the door, a wave of relief washed over me. The worst of this business was behind us. The blame for Marty's death had not, as the killer intended, landed on Angelica's doorstep, and with Moroni's back open, life was returning to normal.

Angelica swung open the door. My heart hammered in my chest as I peered inside. There were the café tables and chairs, the familiar framed prints of Italian tourist sights, and the long glass counter, empty of baked goods. Everything normal.

I let out a long sigh and heard Chief Tedesco do the same.

She and I glanced at each other and smiled ruefully, acknowledging that we'd both expected something bad inside. Another break-in. Another body. A masked killer with a lust for blood.

But Moroni's looked the same as always. In fact, it sparkled and shone in the early morning light.

"Between our search and forensics, we made a mess," Chief Tedesco said. "So we took the liberty of cleaning the bakery for you, Angelica."

"Thank you."

Angelica spun around and threw her arms around the police chief. Chief Tedesco looked bewildered for a moment, unsure where to put her arms, then folded them around Angelica and gave her a pat on the back.

"It was the least we could do," Chief Tedesco said. "Besides, Officers Ferrante and Fontana are a pair of *mammonis*—it doesn't hurt them to practice cleaning up."

We all laughed. I would have loved to have seen Anthony Ferrante, who probably still brought his laundry home to his mother, mopping and scrubbing the bakery.

Inside, Angelica got busy. She put on her apron. We'd

filled Chief Tedesco's cruiser with Tupperware, each one stuffed with dough that Angelica had prepared at home. While I set up the register and added cash, Angelica and Chief Tedesco carried the containers into the back. A moment later, the sounds of the metal trays clanging and the doors of the industrial ovens opening and closing told me that it would be just another day at Moroni's. Exactly as I'd hoped.

I stopped Chief Tedesco on her way out and thanked her.

"Don't thank me yet, Bernie. We haven't caught Marty's killer. Remember, he or she tried to pin this on Angelica. Until we find the right person, there's no telling what they might do."

I looked toward the door to the back. Angelica was humming "That's Amore," which ought to have sent warm waves of joy rippling through my body. Instead, an icy chill leaked down my back. Chief Tedesco was right. The killer was still out there.

"What if it's Rick Alfano?"

"I'm going to track him down," Chief Tedesco said. "I have some questions for him about his time in New York. If we find he was anywhere near Carmine, he'll be our prime suspect, no doubt about that."

After Chief Tedesco left, I arranged the chairs around the café tables. The excitement of reopening Moroni's tingled in my fingertips, and yet I felt unfaithful to Angelica. Because in my heart, I wished I could join Chief Tedesco as she tracked down Rick Alfano to find out where he was the night before Marty's death.

But Angelica and I had plenty of work to do before opening, and soon my mind was preoccupied with pignoli cookies and pizzelles. The counter wouldn't be as well-stocked with cookies and cakes as it usually was, but Angelica was confident we'd catch up during the day.

"Let's open," she said. "Let's bring people back into Moroni's."

I flipped the sign in the window from "Sorry, We're Closed" to "Come In, We're Open," and stood back.

What did I expect, a flash flood of customers knocking me down? Maybe.

No flash flood came.

Angelica and I stood behind the counter. She'd stuffed the ovens with cookies and cakes and loaves of bread. There was nothing to do but wait.

We were still waiting an hour later.

Angelica leaned against the cash register, keeping an ear out for the timers in the bakery and an eye on the door. I sat on a stool with my elbows on the counter and my chin in my hands. Nothing happened. No one came. The buzz I'd felt at reopening had been replaced by a lead-heavy lump in my gut.

"Any moment now, they'll come," Angelica said. "You'll see. Word will spread that we're open again, and they'll come back." She stared at the door. "Won't they?"

At that very moment, the door opened, and the little bell jingled cheerfully. Angelica and I both straightened up.

Nat stood in the entrance. He looked over his shoulder.

"Why do I feel like I'm not who you expected?"

I groaned. "Because you aren't."

One of the timers went off in the bakery and Angelica hurried off to see to the cookies or cake or bread.

Nat approached the counter. "What's going on?"

"Nothing is going on," I said, "and that's the problem. Since opening this morning, we've only had one customer so far. You."

"Well, I'm tickled to be your first. Perhaps if we spread the word…"

He brought out his phone and began texting.

"There," he said, finishing. "I've just suggested subtly that Dan, Joanna, and Phil might want a morning coffee from Moroni's."

Five minutes later, the bell over the door jingled. I was surprised to see Lily, the teenager from Barry Longo's garden party. She was out of her Italian Dream uniform, and instead wore what I supposed was her daily outfit: a t-shirt with a skull on it, baggy cargo pants, and a pair of heavy-looking combat boots. She'd slung a rugged knapsack over her shoulder.

"Hey, Bernie," she said cheerfully. "I was on my way to class, but I had to stop by when I heard you were reopening."

"Did Nat tell you?"

She shook her head. "Joanna did. She's my godmother, and knows all about my—" She bit her lip. "—my obsession with Moroni's."

"You like Moroni's?"

"I love it." A shy smile spread across her face. "Joanna says I should just tell you how I feel, not be so nervous."

"Go ahead then," I said. "Tell me."

"Well, I've been coming here for years, and I've tried just about everything Angelica has ever baked." As she spoke, her shyness gave way to excitement, the words tumbling out. "I haven't been able to visit for months and months because my parents divorced. And for a while, I was living with my dad. And that turned out to be a mess—total drama—so I came back to Carmine. But anyway, my big dream is to learn how to bake like Angelica. I've already been learning. See?"

She interrupted her breathless monologue to dig into

her knapsack. She brought out a notebook and flipped it open, showing me a neatly written recipe.

The header said, "Pizzelle."

She grinned. "They're almost as good as Moroni's."

She flipped to another page. The header said, "Spices."

"Right now, I'm learning all about spices: which ones work well together, what brings out extra flavor, even how to make them myself. At work, we have a food dehydrator, but my boss doesn't let me use it. Which is fine because I do it at home, mostly air-drying, and I've also had luck drying in the refrigerator. The trick is—"

The sound of an oven door shutting in the bakery made Lily look up.

"Wow. Is she back there? Is she baking? What's she making?"

I smiled. Her fangirl enthusiasm was something else. "What can I get you, Lily?"

She ordered a big bag of assorted cookies, then looked at the time on her phone and swore like a sailor, before waving goodbye and hurrying out the door.

After she left, Nat and I looked at each other.

"Wow," he said. "She's like a whirlwind."

"She doesn't lack passion," I agreed, admiring the girl's ambition. Then saw that she'd forgotten her notebook. It lay on the counter.

"Oh, no, she'll be heartbroken to lose this."

I picked it up. It fell open to a blank page. There was no recipe, but Lily had already printed, in her neat hand, what she planned to add: "Mustaccioli."

NAT GRABBED the notebook and rushed out the door, nearly colliding with Dan and Joanna as they walked into Moroni's.

They ordered their favorite coffees to go: Joanna wanted an Americano, Dan a caffe lungo. As I was serving them, the bell jingled softly again, and Phil Palladino joined us.

"What's this about *The Carmine Enquirer* spilling my secrets?"

I stared at him, surprised. "What do you mean?"

At that moment, Nat returned empty-handed, suggesting his mission to return the notebook had been successful. He flipped his floppy hair out of his eyes and tried to catch his breath. Dan put a hand on his shoulder.

"You know, Nat, we love Moroni's. We'll happily come for coffee. Threats really aren't necessary."

"Threats?" I exclaimed. I turned to Nat. "What did you say?"

"Oh, just something about sharing their deepest, darkest secrets with *The Carmine Enquirer*."

I laughed. Fortunately, so did Dan, Joanna, and Phil.

I made them their coffees and Nat lent me a hand.

Standing by the espresso machine, I leaned close to him and whispered, "Did you see the page in Lily's notebook? She was planning to make mustaccioli cookies."

"You said it yourself, Bernie: she was planning to do so. If we'd found a copy of Angelica's own recipe, we'd need to have serious words with Lily."

"I guess you're right..."

"Not everyone is a suspect, you know."

I got busy serving coffee to Dan, Joanna, and Phil.

As they shuffled out of the café, takeout cups in hand, Nat called after them, "Tell your friends: Angelica is innocent, the police are looking at other suspects, and Moroni's is open and safe. Make sure they know that—*it's safe.*"

The door closed.

"What's this about Moroni's being 'safe'?" I asked.

Nat sighed. "Look, gossip can be as poisonous as—as—"

He clearly couldn't come up with an analogy.

"As poisonous as wolfsbane?" I suggested.

"Exactly. There's a story going around that Marty died because of poisoned cookies. Which, of course, he did. But the gossip has grown, and Sofia Ruggiero said she once ate one of Angelica's cookies and got stomach cramps. As the story's spread, Sofia's comment has taken on new meaning."

"Oh, no," I said. "They're staying away because they think Angelica has poisoned more than one person."

Nat nodded. "Unfortunately, yes."

"We need to solve this case."

"True. But until we do, and Angelica is cleared of suspicion, Moroni's could use some good PR."

"But how? Chief Tedesco has already emphasized that Angelica isn't a suspect."

"Sadly, Tedesco has gotten it wrong before, and people know it." He was referring to my moment of fame as a murder suspect. "No, until the police arrest the killer, people will believe the gossip. We need someone with plenty of credibility to vouch for the bakery."

I gave it some thought.

"Like Mayor Blink?"

Nat laughed. "That's funny. No, I said someone with credibility."

"Well, who do you suggest?"

He dug his phone out of his pocket and held it up. He swiped down, scrolling through a social media feed showing posts from three different foodies.

"Jacky Yu, George Pullman, and Molly Messina, three of the hottest food critics in New York right now. All three have reviewed top bakeries. All three have articles or videos about Italian cookies trending on social media. If we could get just one of them to visit and taste Angelica's cookies and talk about them online, Sofia Ruggiero could have a hundred stomach cramps from eating cookies and nobody would care."

I considered his idea. "It's a long shot. But once they try Angelica's baked goods, there's no doubt they'll gush about them."

In the bakery in the back, Angelica was putting more dough in the oven. We told her about the customers who had come, trying to cheer her up.

"Plus, we have an idea for attracting more customers," Nat said, and explained his idea to invite the food critics to Moroni's.

Angelica, covered in flour, listened carefully.

"I don't know..." She sighed. "I've got no experience marketing myself to social media influencers."

"You're in luck," Nat said. "Because I know a bit about it. My ex-boyfriend in New York worked with influencers, and he showed me how he contacted them. I'll help you reach out to them."

Angelica nodded. "All right, then. Let's do it."

While Angelica and Nat settled into her small backroom office, I continued working in the bakery as best I could, and kept an ear out for the front door, in case any customers came. The bell didn't jingle, though, and I had plenty of time to knead dough and decorate cookies.

Half an hour later, Nat and Angelica emerged from the office.

"All done," Nat said, a note of triumph in his voice, and a big smile on his face. "We contacted them all—all three had actual email addresses we could use."

Angelica seemed less buoyant. She got back to her work, bending over the dough and chopping and cutting and shaping with a determination that had a hint of mania in it. After fifteen minutes, she washed her hands and got out her phone.

"What are you doing?" I asked.

"Checking my email to see if they got back to me."

"But Angelica, it could be hours or days before they respond."

"Not so," she said. "An email just came in. It's from Molly Messina."

She read the mail, and gradually the light went out of her eyes. She showed me her phone. The message was brutally short and amounted to "thanks, but no thanks."

She looked miserable. "What if they all say no? What if customers don't come back? How can I stay in business?"

9

By lunchtime, I escaped Angelica's manic pounding and rolling of dough to eat lunch in the park with Nat. We sat on a park bench under a stand of sycamores, eating turkey club sandwiches from Martini's. I put down my sandwich. A familiar figure was creeping along the paths of the park, hunched over and staring at the grass. He had a professional-looking camera on a strap slung around his neck.

I nudged Nat. "What do you think Peter's up to?"

We watched Peter Piatek circle a garbage can with the camera at the ready. He jumped into the gap between two bushes, but emerged looking disappointed.

As he came closer to us, I hailed him.

"What's going on, Peter?"

"I know they're here," he said. "Other people have seen them, but every time I come to take photos, I don't have any luck."

"Leprechauns?" Nat asked.

"Ha, ha, very funny." Peter didn't look amused. "Rats. Phil Palladino said he saw one. So did Sofia Ruggiero."

"Who is a very reliable witness," I said.

Peter shrugged. "She saw what she saw. And I've found some strange information to make the whole story more fishy. For years now, the town council has had an annual contract with an exterminator to provide preemptive pest control. Apparently, Puccini Park has had problems before. The contract was clear. The exterminator had to check on the park—and all other public places, too—and if he found something, he'd get rid of the rats or cockroaches. But see, this is where it gets interesting. Three months ago, the mayor pulled out of the agreement. I spoke with Deputy Mayor Palumbo, and when I asked her about it, she seemed surprised to learn the exterminator had been canceled." He smiled. "I can see the story headline now: 'Ratsy-gate sinks Mayor Blink's reelection.' Good, right?"

"Honestly, it needs work," I said.

"What it needs is a decent photo of a rat," Peter insisted.

He turned and continued his hunt.

My phone pinged. Chief Tedesco had sent me a message. I read the details.

"Chief Tedesco checked Rick Alfano's alibi," I told Nat. "She called the hotel he's staying at and spoke with the staff. They can't corroborate his alibi. Too many people come in and out of the hotel. So, they're pulling security footage to track when he entered the hotel and when he left."

"You think he killed his brother?"

"I don't know," I admitted. "I dislike him, but do I think he'd kill Marty to get his money? It doesn't make much sense. By killing Marty, Rick was only ensuring that Crystal inherited everything. If anyone has a believable motive, it's Barry—he stood to lose everything if Marty told the world he was stealing from clients."

I had the feeling that I was spinning in circles. Was Rick,

who might not have an alibi, even capable of killing his brother? Could Barry somehow have done it, even though he had a solid alibi? And what about the aspiring baker, Lily—did her notebook with the blank entry for mustaccioli make her a suspect?

I crumpled my empty butcher paper, and standing up, threw it in a nearby garbage can.

"Better head back to the bakery. I'm guessing I've got a long afternoon ahead of me with no customers."

"And for once, I really do need to get to work," Nat said, grinning.

We said our goodbyes, and I crossed the wide lawn, heading toward Garibaldi Avenue and Moroni's.

As I approached the path on the other side of the park, I saw another familiar face. It was Barry's sister, whom I'd met at his garden party.

"Hi, Betsy," I called out.

She looked up, and in the same instant, a rat—no doubt startled by my approach—darted out from under a bush, whizzing past her.

She screamed and fluttered her hands. She screamed some more, her eyes bulging with fear. I expected her to bolt in a panic, but she stood rooted to the spot, hands fanning wildly, as she looked back and forth, frantic. Maybe she expected the rat to call reinforcements and overwhelm her.

I jogged up to her.

"It's gone," I said. "Don't worry. There are no more rats."

She stopped screaming. She pressed her hands to her chest. Hyperventilating, she drew in short, shallow breaths. Her eyes remained wide with fear, but after a while, her breathing came in longer and longer intervals.

I put a hand on her arm and said gently, "Hey, are you all right?"

She nodded, tears welling.

"Fear of rats?"

She nodded again. "*Musophobia*."

"I get it," I said.

"You do?"

Her voice was small. Small as a mouse, I thought, but she probably wouldn't appreciate the comparison.

"Personally, rats don't bother me. But snakes..." I shuddered. "Ugh."

"I'm not just afraid of rats, I'm terrified," Betsy said. "Ever since I was a kid...my brother played a mean trick on me..." She took a deep breath. "Anyway, when I see them, I panic and freeze."

I squeezed her arm. "You all right now?"

"I am, thanks."

"Then I'd better get back to work."

I made a move, but Betsy stepped toward me, cutting me off. "Uh, I heard Moroni's is open again. I'm so happy to hear that. Angelica must be thrilled." She smiled, but her smile faltered. "Of course, that's not to say...I mean, it's still horrible about Marty and all."

"Horrible," I agreed.

"But with Moroni's open again, it must mean the police are looking at other suspects."

"That's right."

Chief Tedesco had said that Betsy corroborated Barry's alibi. But I was curious to hear her say it.

"I spoke with your brother. He said he was in New York with you the weekend Marty died."

Betsy nodded. "For my birthday."

"Did you know Marty?"

"He came to some of Barry's parties, but I was always busy working, so we never talked much."

"Did Barry ever talk about Marty?"

"Oh no, never. He talks about the markets and how things are going, but he doesn't talk about his clients. He respects their privacy. Barry is a good man, he really is. He wouldn't hurt a fly."

I cocked my head, studying her. "Why do you say that?"

Betsy got flustered. "Well, no reason. I mean..." She seemed to straighten up, making a visible effort to be strong. "Look, Bernie, I know you visited him. He told me. And I'm no idiot. I know why you're asking questions. You didn't go to Barry to get financial advice. You went to snoop."

"Me, snoop?" I said as innocently as I could.

"You've helped the police before—in the Mark Lewis and Johnny Greco murders—it's no secret. Everyone knows that you're still playing Eve Silver."

"All right, maybe I was snooping. I was curious about why Marty accused Barry of stealing."

It was a long shot. I wanted to see how Betsy reacted.

Betsy's face flushed bright red. "Who told you?"

I shrugged. "A friend of Marty's."

"It was a misunderstanding, that's all. Marty had promised not to tell anyone. They were working it out." Her breaths were quick and shallow again. "Barry would never —it was about money, that's all. He was going to pay Marty back, and Marty was going to forget the whole thing. Barry would never, ever, ever kill anyone. You've got to believe me."

She grabbed my arm.

"Please, believe me..."

"I believe you," I said, and saw the relief spread across her face.

But did I believe her? If Barry was so innocent, why did his sister need to defend him?

10

F riday. The day of Marty's funeral. Overnight, northeasterly gusts had swept away summer. Carlo's Restaurant lay only a few steps from Moroni's, but as I hurried down the sidewalk, carrying a tray of cannolis, I shivered in the cool morning wind.

On Carmine's iron lampposts, the decorative metal baskets with flowers swung and clattered. A plastic bag sailed down the street. A raindrop hit my cheek.

It was a relief to enter the warm, cozy interior of Carlo's. As usual, the carpeted floors, heavy drapes, and gentle jazz created a kind of cocoon—a perfect escape in which to relish Carlo's delicious Italian food. The smell of lasagna and sausage and peppers filled the room. Lunchtime patrons already occupied most tables.

Carlo, seeing me from afar, gestured wildly for me to hurry. I handed him the tray of cannolis, and he passed them over the bar to Maria Ferrante—Anthony's sister. She gave me a smile. Even though Anthony and I had broken up, Maria still liked me. If anything, she liked me more.

"Hey, Bernie—how're things at the bakery?" she asked.

"Bad. Several people came this morning, just like yesterday, but a few sympathy visits won't be enough to keep Moroni's in business."

Carlo shushed us, cutting off the conversation. He leaned close to me and whispered in my ear.

"Over there," he hissed.

I looked around the restaurant at the people eating lunch.

"The guy eating linguini," I asked, "the one who looks like a professor?"

The man with a bushy, gray mustache wore a tweed jacket and thick horn-rimmed glasses. A hardbound book lay open on the table, so he could read while he was eating.

"No, not him. Over by the window."

I saw a young woman carefully eating a scallop. I didn't recognize her as a local.

"So? It's a customer from out of town."

"'So'? I'll tell you 'so.' She's Jacky Yu, the famous food vlogger."

The word vlogger sounded strange coming from Carlo's lips. He wasn't a tech whiz, nor particularly interested in pop culture or social media. But apparently he'd done his homework. In a breathless whisper, he mentioned the many restaurants whose reputations Jacky Yu had sent skyrocketing to stardom.

"Has she said anything about the food, Carlo?"

"Said anything about the food?" Carlo sounded affronted. "Of course, she hasn't. She's been too busy savoring it."

I had an idea. "Mind if I talk to her?"

I explained how Nat had helped Angelica reach out to Jacky and other food critics, and Carlo was thrilled.

"Yes, of course. I bet that is why she's here. Bernie, you

need to talk to her. See if you can get her to visit my sister. And to help persuade her, I'll give her a complimentary cannoli."

I headed over to Jacky's table.

"Jacky Yu?"

She looked up at me and smiled. "Hi—do you follow my channel?"

"My name's Bernie and I work next door at Moroni's Italian Bakery and—"

She cocked her head, studying me. "Wait a minute, I know you. Oh, my God, you're that actress who went into witness protection. You played Eve Silver."

"That's right." Maybe my previous life as a celebrity would come in handy. "I'm happy to appear in one of your videos if you want to shoot over at the bakery."

But Jacky shook her head.

"Sorry, I can't," she said. "I've heard about the scandal."

"Scandal?"

"The murder. The poisoned cookies."

"The police don't see Angelica Moroni as a suspect, and the bakery is open for business again."

"I don't know...I have a reputation to protect, and if my personal brand gets mixed up in this..."

"Look," I said. "All you have to do is go to Moroni's and try the cookies. If you like them, you can shoot a video. If you don't, you can drop it, and you won't risk anything."

She thought for a moment. Then nodded. "All right, I'll do it. A good bakery deserves exposure, and if what I hear about Moroni's is true, the cookies are better than good. I'll drop by after lunch."

A thrill tingled in my hands. Jacky was sure to love Moroni's. But then I remembered the funeral, and my heart sank.

"Uh, well, actually, we're closed after lunch for a funeral. But how about afterward? At the end of the afternoon?"

She checked her phone, swiping through her calendar app. "I guess...but I've got to be back in New York City tonight."

"See you later, then," I said. "Enjoy your lunch."

She speared another scallop. "I will—it's excellent."

Phew. My feet felt lighter as I walked away from her. With a positive review from Jacky Yu, her millions of followers would take note. They would want to check out Moroni's, and that would help the bakery restore its reputation. I only hoped Jacky showed up.

As I turned to the door, intending to hurry back to tell Angelica the excellent news, I froze.

At one of the tables sat Rick Alfano.

He was seated against the wall, eating spaghetti with clam sauce and reading something off a tablet. He scrolled with one hand and corkscrewed spaghetti onto his fork with the other. As he shoved the food in his mouth, clam sauce splashed his white button-down shirt.

"Aw, come on, man—"

He cursed, put down his fork, and pushed back his chair. He headed for the restroom at the back, leaving a wake of R-rated language behind him. Apparently, HerbaTroo didn't provide a remedy for a filthy mouth.

On the chair across from Rick's sat a white paper bag with "Vitale's Cookies" on the side. I knew that name. It was the famous Italian bakery in New York City that had been featured in videos by Jacky Yu and others. Now, why was Rick Alfano carrying around a bag of cookies from Vitale's?

Under different circumstances, it wouldn't be suspicious. But Rick had access to the poison that killed Marty. So far, he didn't have a solid alibi. The question was how he'd gotten the cookies to replace Angelica's. Could the answer be in that bag?

I crept over to the table. I glanced around. Carlo was watching me with a wide-eyed what-the-heck-are-you-doing look, but I ignored him. Trying to look surreptitious, I opened the bag and peeked inside.

I gasped.

Jackpot.

Inside the paper bag were half a dozen chocolate-covered cookies.

Mustaccioli.

Marty's favorite. And the killer's murder weapon.

By the time the funeral procession left St. Joseph's Catholic Church, it was raining steadily. The church stood at the end of Puccini Park. The cemetery wasn't far, but it lay on a hill above town—appropriately called Cypress Hill—and the pallbearers loaded Marty's coffin into the hearse for the short drive up to the grave.

Chief Tedesco offered me a ride, but Angelica wanted to walk, and I joined her. She'd been cheerful after the news about Jacky Yu dropping by to taste her cookies, but now she was somber. And who could blame her? We'd sat through a long funeral mass with prayers and readings about resurrection and judgment day, and although much of it was beautiful, none of it suggested anything personal about Marty. I'd expected a speech by Rick, but interestingly, both he and Crystal had left the talking to the priest.

Angelica and I walked in silence, heading up the street to the cemetery.

I soon regretted the decision to walk. Whenever I

convinced myself the weather wasn't so bad, the wind gusted and tossed a handful of hard rain against my face.

Angelica and I trudged through the cemetery's massive wrought-iron gate and up the winding path that led to Marty's plot.

Marty's headstone was impossible to miss. Even at a distance, it stood out. Up close, it towered over us, looking like a monument to a king. No doubt Marty had hoped for that effect. Engraved on the headstone were the words, "*Sequere Pecuniam*." I guessed it was Latin, but had no idea what it meant.

"It was Marty's favorite Latin phrase," Angelica explained. "It means 'follow the money.'"

A crowd had already gathered around the open grave. In *Silver & Gold*, Eve Silver and Adam Gold had often shown up at funerals to see how the suspects reacted. In the show, the detectives always had a revelation—or at least a new clue emerged.

I studied the people gathered.

Crystal was there, of course, a hand pressed behind one hip, as if her pregnant belly was causing her pain. She wore a black dress and, sensibly, a raincoat. Many other familiar faces ringed the grave: Chief Tedesco, Dan Russo, Joanna Parisi (her husband Gino, as always, was absent on business), Phil Palladino, Sofia Ruggiero, Rose Calabrese, and Primo Leone. Curiosity rather than grief must have brought them.

Nat broke away from the crowd and joined us. Just then, the wind drove a sheet of rain over the hill, splattering us all.

"The weather is perfect for a funeral," he said.

"Honestly, sunshine would have been fine," I said, "especially since no one looks sad."

"Well, not exactly 'no one.'"

I saw what he was referring to. The people from Carmine didn't look downcast. But scattered throughout the crowd were several unfamiliar women in black. Out-of-towners. Most looked weepy. One was outright sobbing, while another gritted her teeth as tears trickled down her face, her fists clenched as she stared daggers at the hole in the ground.

Anthony Ferrante stood next to the woman sobbing. He handed her a tissue and put an arm around her shoulders.

I shook my head. *Nothing like a funeral for hitting on women, eh, Anthony?*

How had I not seen what a bad match Anthony and I really were? It wasn't love. Maybe I'd been a little desperate to find a lover. My life had been a mess for a long time—could I blame myself for wanting the comfort of a little romance?

"Do you know who that chick is?" Crystal appeared at my side. She was gesturing at the woman Anthony was comforting. "And that one? And the other one over there—the one who looks like she'd be happy to murder Marty if he were still alive?"

I shrugged. "Friends of Marty's?" Then I understood. "Oh, I see..."

"Right," Crystal said.

"What?" Nat asked. "What am I missing?"

"Those young women all had affairs with Marty." Crystal's face soured into a grimace. "Or I guess Marty had affairs with them."

"Oh," Nat said. "Now I see, too."

The priest arrived, followed by the pallbearers. They lowered the coffin into the ground. The priest read from the Bible, from Corinthians.

As I studied their faces, people joined in reciting the

Prayer for the Dead ("Deliver them now from every evil, and bid them eternal rest...").

One pallbearer attracted most of my attention: Rick Alfano.

The priest said a few words and then nodded to Rick, who stepped up to the grave. It seemed he was finally going to make his speech. He held open a piece of paper with notes on it, and the wind tugged at it.

"My brother, Marty, was a good man. Smart, fair, and generous." He looked around at the gathering, as if willing anyone to defy his words. His gaze landed on Crystal. "Especially generous. He and I had a rocky relationship. The Alfanos have always been headstrong. Driven. Visionary. Building a business from scratch. Changing the way people live through body-enhancing herbal supplements. Homeopathic remedies that can bring joy to the mind and the soul."

I groaned inwardly. Was he making a speech for his dead brother or advertising his business?

"Through all the years," he continued, "Marty always said to me—whenever we had a chance to catch up—that despite our disagreements, I would always be his brother. He had my back, and I had his. If anything should ever happen to one of us..."

He gazed at the grave, clearly trying to look bereaved. He was a terrible actor.

"If one of us should die first, we made a vow to take care of the other. What was mine was his, and what was his was..." Again, he looked at Crystal. "...mine."

Crystal leaned close to me and said, "Don't worry, he's not in love with me, just my money."

"*Sequere pecuniam*," Rick said. "Brother, I will honor your wishes and follow the money."

He leaned down and picked something up—the white paper bag I'd seen in the restaurant—and he grabbed a handful of cookies and flung them onto the coffin below.

"Rest in peace," he said as he flung another cookie with surprising force, and it smashed against the coffin.

The priest wrapped up the proceedings, and many of the mourners repeated the last prayer after him. Then he said, "Ashes to ashes, dust to dust..."

Through it all, Angelica had remained dry-eyed. But now she let out a long, shuddering sigh.

"You all right?" I whispered to her.

"What a bitter ending to a bitter man's life. I need something extra sweet."

"You going straight back to the bakery?"

She nodded. "I need to feel the soft dough between my fingers and smell the sugar baking in the ovens. There's nothing more restorative. Plus, I want to make sure Moroni's is open when Jacky Yu passes by."

She gave me a smile, and it warmed my heart: as long as she had Moroni's, Angelica was going to be all right.

With the funeral over, the crowd dispersed, mourners ducking under their coats and hurrying back to their cars in the nearby parking lot.

Rick hurried to Crystal and took her arm.

"Allow me," he said. "It can't be easy to carry all that weight."

"Drop it, Rick." Crystal pulled her arm away. "You're never getting that money. Ever."

Rick's jaw clenched, the little muscles on the sides of his face dancing angrily.

"You'd better reconsider..." His voice had dropped to a low, menacing whisper. "Don't cross me..."

Crystal smiled. "Richard Alfano, you know what you can do with your threats and your herbal supplements...?"

The wind rose into a banshee-like howl, and for an instant, I missed what Crystal said next, but apparently it wasn't nice. Rick's face turned beet red, and he spun around and stomped off.

He moved quickly. But not quickly enough to escape me. I was almost jogging to keep up with him. "Can I just say that the cookies were a nice touch, Rick? But I'm guessing this was the first time you brought Marty his favorite cookies. The two of you didn't get along."

Rick came to a dead stop, allowing Crystal and the others to stream past us. The two of us were alone. He leaned close, jabbing a finger in my face. "You listen to me, Eve Silver. I know what you're insinuating. Yeah, I may not have gone to Carmine or Short Hills to visit my brother. I may not have talked to him for years. But that doesn't mean we didn't have an understanding."

"An understanding that you ought to inherit?"

"The money belongs to me, not that—that—"

"Choose your words carefully, mister. Crystal is my friend."

He let out a growl and stalked off.

"What was that about?" Chief Tedesco asked, coming up to me.

I repeated what Rick had said. "If we're to believe him, he never went near Marty."

"His story checks out, Bernie. The manager of the hotel in New York City shared the security footage. The night before Marty died, Rick went to his room at 11 pm and didn't emerge until 7 am the next morning. He might be a lousy brother—even a crappy human being—but his alibi is airtight."

I let out a sigh. How I wanted Rick to be the killer. Seeing him in handcuffs would have been a special treat. But even if he had superpowers and climbed down the side of the hotel, he couldn't have made it to Carmine in time to swap the cookies, send the email, and call Marty. We'd have to cross him off the list of suspects.

"If Rick didn't do it, who is our primary suspect?"

Chief Tedesco shrugged. "No one."

We stood in the whipping rain for a long time, going back over the details of the case, details we'd already reviewed again and again: the break-in, the missing keys and notebook, the poison, the messages to Marty and Angelica, the swapping of cookies. The cemetery was empty, everyone having gone by the time we'd picked over the facts.

"Rick has an alibi, and so does Barry," I said. "Still, there's something fishy about Barry Longo and his investments."

"I agree. We'd better take a closer look at Barry and see—"

Chief Tedesco's radio strapped to her shoulder crackled to life, and a voice spoke in rapid fire sentences.

"Chief. Officer Fontana here. We found a body…"

"Where? Who?"

"At Moroni's Italian Bakery."

I gasped. "Angelica—is she all right?"

Chief Tedesco shushed me, so she could hear what Officer Fontana said next.

"Chief, it's that financial adviser. It's Barry Longo. He's dead."

11

B arry Longo, wearing a pair of purple chinos and a white shirt with purple polka dots, lay slumped over a café table. He had died in the same spot as Marty.

But there was a key difference.

"No cookies," was the first thing Chief Tedesco said when we walked into the bakery.

There was no plate with poisoned cookies on the table-top. A lone cup of coffee stood, half empty, next to a pink sticky note. I came close, keeping my hands in my pockets to avoid the temptation of touching anything, a trick I'd learned on the set of *Silver & Gold*.

"That's one of the pink sticky notes Angelica keeps in her office," I said.

On the note, a hasty hand had scrawled,

Thanks for coming, Barry. Be right with you. I made coffee, please enjoy.
Angelica.

Chief Tedesco crouched down to inspect Barry without touching him.

"I bet he was poisoned, like Marty," she said.

"Coffee instead of cookies?"

"Exactly. What do you make of the note?"

I studied the handwriting more closely. It tilted slightly to the left. In an episode of *Silver & Gold*, Eve Silver and Adam Gold had solved a murder by matching the handwriting to the killer's personality. A graphologist had advised them on the show that the left-slanting handwriting suggested a person who was emotionally repressed and withdrawn. Whether that was true or not, the handwriting on this note didn't match Angelica's looping style.

"Definitely not Angelica's," I told Chief Tedesco.

She gave a curt nod. Then gestured for me to follow her outside.

Angelica was sitting on the fender of Chief Tedesco's car, a blanket over her shoulders and a mug of coffee in her hands, courtesy of Carlo. He stood by her side. The lights from the police cruiser flashed on his face, making his eyes look even more darkened with worry.

"I'm all right," she assured her brother. "Shocked, but all right."

When she caught sight of Chief Tedesco, she shrugged the blanket off her shoulders and handed the mug to Carlo. She took a step toward us. "Chief, you don't think I killed Barry, did you?"

Chief Tedesco frowned. "Tell me exactly what happened."

Angelica had left us at the cemetery and caught a ride with Nat, who'd dropped her off at the bakery before heading back to his work at the public library and historical society.

"I unlocked the front door…"

"You're sure it was locked?" Chief Tedesco asked.

"I'm sure," she said. "I locked it myself when I left, and it was locked when I got back."

Chief Tedesco nodded. "Go ahead, continue."

"There's not much else to say. I opened the door and stepped inside and there he was, sitting on the chair with his head on the table, like he was sleeping. I stepped outside and dialed 9-1-1." She eyed Chief Tedesco, nervously. "Tell me, do you really believe I killed him?"

"I'm an idiot," Chief Tedesco said, looking grim. "The killer still has your extra keys. We should have changed those locks at once. But I'm not so big an idiot that I believe this clumsy attempt to pin Barry's death on you. I've watched enough episodes of *Silver & Gold* to know when someone is being framed."

Angelica put a hand to her chest. "Oh, what a relief. I was so worried you believed…"

Chief Tedesco held up a hand, stopping Angelica. "You may not enjoy hearing what I have to say next. I don't believe you killed Barry Longo, any more than you killed Marty Alfano. You were at the funeral and then with Nat until the body was discovered. You wouldn't have had enough time to serve Barry a poisoned cup of coffee. Your alibi is good."

"It's rock solid," I said, and took one of Angelica's hands in mine and gave it a squeeze.

Angelica smiled at my show of support.

"Still, I've got to go by the book," Chief Tedesco continued. "And going by the book means bringing you in for questioning, Angelica. But that's not the bad news." She drew in a breath and exhaled. "Since Barry presumably died from poisoning at your premises, I have no choice…"

"No," I said with a groan.

Angelica's face had turned chalk white.

"I'm sorry," Chief Tedesco said. "I'll have to close the bakery again."

~

"THIS IS A DISASTER," Carlo said miserably.

We watched the police cruisers drive away, one of them carrying Angelica in the back. The coroner and forensics teams had come and gone. Moroni's windows were dark, the front door yet again sealed with yellow crime scene tape.

"Just when Angelica was feeling more hopeful, this happens," I said. "We can only pray the police get the lab results they need, so the bakery can open as soon as possible."

He shook his head. "It won't be in time for the Italian Day Celebration."

I put a hand to my cheek. How could I forget? Angelica and Carlo were supposed to be the stars of the Italian Day Celebration in Puccini Park. That was tomorrow—the bakery would never be open in time.

The wind shook the crime tape across Moroni's front door, and I hugged myself against the cold.

"Hi again!" a voice said behind me. "Can we get out of this horrible weather? I've got exactly 30 minutes before I need to drive back to the city."

I turned, my heart sinking. Jacky Yu had dressed for warmer weather, and she shivered as she tugged her long, soft-knit cardigan across her chest. I'd forgotten all about her visit, and here she was, ready to sample Moroni's famous baked goods.

She frowned. "Why's the bakery closed? Wait a minute, is that crime scene tape?"

"Uh..."

"I thought the bakery was open again."

"It was..." I said, trying to think fast.

There was no knowing whether we'd ever entice the vlogger back to distant Carmine. I had to get her to try Angelica's baked goods. It would be a small ray of sunlight on an otherwise dark day.

"If you hang around, I'm sure Angelica Moroni will be done at the police station soon, and she can share some of her cookies with you. She's got a ton at home."

"Police station?" Jacky sounded alarmed. "What's happened? Another murder? Oh, no. This stuff makes me super nervous, and anyway, I've gotta go."

She held up her hands in a gesture of surrender, spun around, and then hurried off.

I buried my head in my hands. "This couldn't get any worse..."

A man cleared his throat, and I looked up.

"Mayor Blink," Carlo said, surprised.

"I heard the horrific news about Barry, and came as quickly as I could."

His face was flushed, and he wheezed as he tried to catch his breath. His expression of shock seemed believable. He looked pale and sweaty, and he tugged at his collar to loosen his tie.

"Let me get straight to the point. The thing is, Carlo, with a second murder at Moroni's, there's too much bad publicity going around."

"But Angelica is innocent," Carlo said.

"I know, I know." Mayor Blink swept a hand across his brow, wiping perspiration away. He glanced over his shoulder, as if he worried someone was watching him. "But I must put the wellbeing of Carmine first, and so I've decided to pass the catering duties to another vendor."

I clenched my fists and stepped toward him. "You what?"

"Young lady—"

"Call me 'lady' again in that patronizing way and I swear I'll explode."

"With the bakery closed, catering for the Italian Day Celebration is uncertain. I need to make sure the festivities go off without a hitch tomorrow."

I thought of Peter's investigation into the mayor's shady dealings. It might be my anger affecting my brain, but I could swear I smelled a rat. Hadn't he also canceled the exterminator contract on his own, without consulting the deputy mayor or any of the many town council committees?

"Who did you give the contract to?"

"The company's called Italian Dream, and they've assured me that—"

The words were out of my mouth before I could restrain myself: "And how many dollars did it take to 'assure' you?"

Mayor Blink's bright red face got a shade paler. "I never...how dare you...? I could sue you for slander. I could—"

Carlo grabbed me just as I was about to launch myself at the rat.

Mayor Blink backed away. He seemed to gather himself and straightened his tie. "Look, Italian Dream will ensure that visitors to Carmine don't leave with a bad taste in their mouth, and I have to do what's right for the town. I have to do what's right."

He hurried away, fleeing from my anger.

"I have to do what's right," he called over his shoulder, casting a worried, hunted look back at me.

We watched Mayor Blink jog down the sidewalk, then jaywalk across Garibaldi Avenue to the municipal building.

"Coward."

"He is that," Carlo said with a sigh. "And much worse. But there's nothing we can do about it, Bernie. We've run out of time and options."

He stepped inside his restaurant, his feet dragging, as if he were bone weary, and a moment later, I saw him in the window among the heavy drapes. He grabbed the edge of the sign that proudly announced that Carlo's Restaurant and Moroni's Italian Bakery would be providing delicious food and baked goods at the annual Italian Day Celebration. Then he ripped it free from the tape, leaving a big gap in the window.

I stared up at the dark sky, willing it to rain down. At least a deluge would be cathartic. But it didn't rain. Instead, the clouds, playing a cruel trick, parted and revealed the last rays of the setting sun.

12

"Mayor Blink's guilty," Peter said.

Nat frowned. "Mayor Blink murdered Marty and Barry?"

Four of us sat in a booth at the Old Mill that evening: Peter, Crystal, Nat, and me. Jerry had made three Campari and sodas—one each for Nat, Peter, and me—and a mocktail for Crystal with cranberry and lemon juice and a secret ingredient. Tonight's special drinks were all green, white, or red, like the Italian flag, a celebration of the town's cultural heritage.

"No, no, the mayor didn't kill anyone," Peter said, shaking his drink so the ice cubes rattled. "I'm saying he's guilty of fraud, embezzlement, something. I've looked at the municipal budget, and there are several things that don't add up. The exterminator contract was canceled. So was a landscaping agreement and other services. But none of the items were removed from the town council's budget, as if Carmine were still paying. And now the mayor suddenly yanks the Italian Day contract from under Carlo and Angelica's feet? I mean, look, I could see saying that Moroni's can't manage it. But why not keep Carlo and outsource the baking to another vendor?"

"Maybe no competitor would want the contract without the full kit and caboodle," Nat suggested. "Italian Dream is an events-and-catering company and offers both dessert and savory food. Simply doing the desserts might not be lucrative enough."

"Or perhaps Bernie is right, and Mayor Blink got a bribe, or even demanded it."

Peter and Nat turned to me. Through the discussion, I'd sat slumped down in my seat, sipping my drink as my mind ran in circles around the case.

I put down my glass. "I honestly don't know what to think, but I agree with you, Peter. I smell a rat."

Peter nodded. "And it's not just the ones overrunning Puccini Park."

"Marty's dead and now Barry, too," I said. "And that only leaves Rick Alfano..."

"You'd better forget about Rick Alfano," Crystal said. "Because I've got bad news for you, sweetie. He's gone. He told me he'd be catching an evening flight back home. By now, he's in the air, en route to Los Angeles."

"I guess it doesn't matter," I said. "Chief Tedesco said his alibi checked out..."

Unless...

I sat up. "What if Rick somehow tricked the security cameras and left the hotel? And what if he killed Barry before the funeral? Angelica and I walked to the cemetery, which would have given him time to enter Moroni's, murder Barry, and then slip out in time to join the funeral."

"Nice theory," Crystal said. "Only one problem with it: someone can vouch for Rick's whereabouts before the funeral."

"Who?"

"Me." Crystal sighed. "Rick came to my parents' house, saying he wanted to comfort me and escort me to the funeral, how hard it must be for me, especially when I was pregnant, blah, blah, blah. Really, he wanted me to promise I'd share the money. A slice of the pie. He threatened to take me to court if I didn't give up the inheritance."

"What a classy guy," Nat said.

"Yeah, a real angel. But angel or devil, he stuck to me like glue. It wasn't until I told him for the third time—after we'd left Marty's grave—that I would never, ever pay him. Then he got the message and bolted. So, you see, Bernie, he's a piece of dirt, but he couldn't have killed Barry."

I slumped down in my seat again. Barry didn't kill Marty and Rick didn't kill Barry, and everyone had an airtight alibi. We were back at square one. I took a big gulp of my drink.

"WAKE UP AND SMELL THE COFFEE," Jay Casanova said, grinning at me. "It's poisoned."

In my dream, I was holding in one hand a half-eaten cannoli shell in my hand, the ricotta cream as red as blood —in the other, an empty coffee cup.

I woke with a start.

Early morning light streamed through my curtains. Somehow, I'd coiled my bedsheet into a thick rope and woven it around my left leg. I untangled myself and slipped over the edge of the bed.

I rubbed my face with my hands and groaned. What a terrible night. Nightmare after nightmare had woken me, and I felt as if I'd slept only a few hours.

Coffee, I thought.

I wriggled my feet into my fluffy bunny slippers and was about to head to the kitchen when I froze.

Coffee. I smelled coffee.

I didn't have an automatic coffee maker, preferring an Italian stovetop moka pot that could make strong espressos. Unless a fairy had arrived this morning to magically brew me coffee, something was very wrong.

I looked around my bedroom for a weapon. The only decent object was my bedtime reading: a hardback copy of Raymond Chandler's *Farewell, My Lovely*.

It was big. It was blunt. It would have to do.

With the Chandler book raised over my head—it really was heavy—I tiptoed out of my bedroom and down the short hallway, my bunny slippers muting my steps.

Ahead of me, the kitchen came partially into view, but only the fridge and the row of cupboards.

I pressed my back against the wallpaper, listening.

A clink, like the tap of a spoon—or more likely a sharp, murderous knife—made my heart skip a beat. My breath sounded unnaturally loud in my ears.

I waited a few beats.

Don't wait too long, I told myself. *Gotta catch the intruder unawares.*

I drew in a deep breath. Then swiveled around the corner, raising the Chandler to throttle whoever had broken into my home.

My guest was sitting at my kitchen table, calmly stirring sugar into an espresso cup.

"Are you lending me that book," she said, "or are you about to clobber me with it?"

I lowered the Chandler.

"Roberta."

"Bernie."

I exhaled, relieved. At the kitchen table, I put down the book. Roberta LaRosa picked up the moka pot and poured me a cup of coffee. She pushed it across the tabletop toward me.

"Sugar?"

I sat down and shook my head, eyeing the small bowl of cane sugar cubes, which I kept for guests.

"Since when do you use sugar?"

"These are hard times."

I took a sip of coffee, welcoming the jolt to my heart and brain.

"Why are you here? And why have you been snooping around Carmine?"

"Friendly visit."

"Wait a minute..."

The coffee was working. Bells were going off in my head, and I began to revisit the times I'd spotted Roberta. Twice. And each time outside the same house.

The realization struck me hard. "You weren't spying on me. You were spying on Barry Longo."

Roberta raised her cup, as if she were toasting me. "Bravo. I'd better tell you what I know."

She began a story, both longwinded and vague, about a friend she had in the FBI, and how he happened to keep her informed about investigations in and around Carmine, New Jersey.

"He understands I take a special interest in the town. Never mind why," she added, silencing my questions. "What you need to know is that the feds have been watching Barry Longo for a while."

"They were staking out Barry's house, too? But I only saw you, no one else."

She grimaced. "They have more practice at hiding in

plain sight than I do. There were a couple of them at the party, undercover as investment clients. Since I wasn't officially working the case, I had to stick to the sidelines."

"The feds were onto something," I said. "He's been stealing from his clients."

"It's worse than that. Barry started small. A little Ponzi scheme, where he'd pay out big sums to impress people and attract more clients. A little skimming from his most successful customers. Making 'reinvestments' that would conveniently vanish into an offshore account. With this experience, he soon got drafted into the Major Leagues."

"Organized crime?"

She nodded. "Money laundering for the mafia."

She reached down next to her chair and pulled up a laptop bag. The manila file folder she removed was thick. It was also plain and unmarked.

"If anyone asks, this folder fell off a truck. You didn't get it from me. In fact, I was never here. But I figure I can share it with you, since Barry's dead, and the feds will be closing the case."

She pushed it across the table to me.

I opened it. Inside were reams of paper with reports from stakeouts of Barry's home, lists of visitors to his house, surveillance transcripts of conversations, phone records, a heap of photos catching the man himself at his home, on the street, even shopping at Martini's Italian Market. I saw a photo of myself standing near Barry at his garden party and winced. I looked so underdressed compared to everyone else. Should I be making more of an effort? Maybe I ought to replace some of my old jeans and get something besides t-shirts and hoodies.

"What is it you see?" Roberta asked. "A clue?"

"A clue to why I'm still single."

I flipped onward to the next photo. This one was of Barry and another familiar face: Marty Alfano. They were sitting on Barry's patio, both wearing sunglasses in the sunshine, with laptops open on a table and ice coffees in their hands.

"Was Marty Alfano implicated?"

Roberta shook her head. "Nothing shady about his finances. In fact, there's a transcript of a conversation in the packet where Marty all but accuses Barry of stealing."

I found the transcript and read it. The conversation had occurred two days before the garden party. Marty made it clear in no uncertain terms that if Barry didn't make the money reappear, he'd go to the authorities.

BARRY: No need for that, buddy.

MARTY: I'm not your buddy, Longo. And I won't be your client much longer. Transfer the money you owe me and I'll walk away. If you don't, I'll call the cops.

BARRY: Let's not get excited. We can work this out.

MARTY: I've said all there is to say.

I reread that last part, the words sparking a memory. Where had I heard Marty say that? Oh, yes. The garden party. When I'd gone to the bathroom, I'd overheard Marty speaking with someone in the garden, telling them more or less the same thing. Only the person had threatened him. Could it have been Barry?

I shook my head. Once again, I was going in circles. Even if Barry had felt threatened by Marty, he'd been nowhere near Carmine on the weekend of his client's death, and now he had the ultimate alibi: he was dead.

I flipped through the pages and the photos. The snapshot of myself caught my attention again. Barry was sipping his cocktail. At the edge of the photo, I could see Marty and Crystal—Crystal looking miserable—and Mayor Blink, on his own. He clutched a lobster roll in his hand as he scowled at Barry. The blurred background included one of the catering staff, whose face was a smudge. The rest of the photo was a riot of colors, the bright flowers creating a vibrant, unfocused backdrop. Of all the photos, this one felt the most important, and it wasn't because of my disappointing fashion choices. But why did the photo tug at something in my brain?

A list of phone calls, incoming and outgoing, to Barry's home caught my attention. His landline showed dozens of calls to and from Mayor Blink. A few with Marty, too, including one the day before he died. After that, there was an incoming call that stood out: it was from Phil Palladino.

"Must be a mistake..." I mumbled to myself because the time of the call seemed odd. I looked up at Roberta. "Would a person's number be logged on this sheet if they called, but no one answered?"

"Sure." She leaned over the table and pointed a finger at the sheet. "Check that column for the duration of the call."

"This says the call lasted 2.5 minutes." I thought about that. "But it was the middle of the night. It must have been a long voicemail."

I moved on. There were pages and pages of financial tallies, with commentary by the FBI explaining the meaning of Barry's many money movements. One stood out.

"Wait a minute," I said. "This suggests that the town council was paying Barry Longo for his services."

"Uh-huh."

I gave a low whistle. "And his services were *expensive*."

"You can say that again."

As I kept reading, the ugly truth emerged. Mayor Blink

had been draining the town coffers, feeding Barry the funds that should have gone to exterminators, the public library, and the historical society, even the bus service to bring kids to the nearest school in the district. Between them, Blink and Barry had been bleeding Carmine dry.

"How did they think they could get away with this?"

"You'll see in the transcripts that Barry expected a windfall from his work with the mafia, and that would allow Mayor Blink to plug the gaps. Several times, Barry tells Blink, 'Don't worry, I'll plug the gaps.' The mayor's a greedy fool. He didn't know what he was doing. Barry seemed more savvy."

"So why haven't the feds arrested the mayor yet?"

"Mayor Blink is small fry. They'll leave him to Chief Tedesco. The feds wanted Barry's connections to the mob, and right before he was killed, they'd approached him. He denied everything, of course. Then, when they made it clear they had concrete evidence to nail him, he said he had valuable information, too. He wanted a trade. He wanted leniency. But it wasn't about the mafia."

I snorted. "What could he possibly give the feds that would help his case?"

"It was about a murder."

"Murder?"

Roberta nodded.

"He was going to tell them who killed Marty Alfano."

13

The sign in the window of Milano Books said, "Happy Italian Day!" I'd nearly forgotten that today was the big celebration in Puccini Park. Next to the sign was another: "Sorry, We're Closed."

I leaned close to the window and narrowed my eyes, staring past the display of paperbacks and into the store. Within, a shadowy figure moved out of the stacks.

I knocked on the door. The shadow stopped moving. A moment later, he walked to the door and came into focus: Phil Palladino.

He unlocked the door and opened it wide, smiling.

"Bernie, how ya doin'?"

Phil was wearing his usual corduroy pants, Oxford button-down, and cardigan. Even in warm weather, he wore cardigans.

"We open in—" He checked his watch. "—15 minutes."

"I know," I said. "But I've got to talk to you."

After parting ways with Roberta, I'd gone back over the FBI file, and I'd been struck by this: Barry had dozens of incoming and outgoing calls from Mayor Blink, even a few with Marty, and then one from Phil Palladino.

In the middle of the night. Hours before Marty would die.

Phil ushered me inside, closing the door behind me.

Milano Books was a delight: wooden shelves along all the walls, display tables with neatly arranged paperbacks and hardcovers, small handwritten cards everywhere with notes on why a book deserved to be read. There were even a couple of armchairs and a small couch for patrons to sit in and flip through a book, encouraging them to take their time to decide what to buy.

I smiled. "A bookstore is one of the best places on the planet."

"You know I won't dispute that statement. A book is the closest we humans come to conjuring, so a bookstore is actually a magic store. No secret trapdoors or hidden rabbits, though. Just the miracle of words."

As he mused on the joys of books, his eyes focused on something far away in the distance, his voice took on a dreamy quality and his face lit up with a smile.

I interrupted his daydream.

"I was wondering about the garden party at Barry Longo's..."

"May he rest in peace," Phil said, grimacing.

I couldn't come straight out and say that I knew he'd called Barry. If he asked how I knew that, I had no good excuse. I had to tread carefully.

"Sometimes the noise from Barry's home bothered you..."

"Sometimes? There was always noise. Barry was a nuisance. He was so loud—" Phil caught himself. "Oh, I probably shouldn't vent my frustrations, not now that he's dead."

"I need to know something. On the night before Marty died, the night between Friday and Saturday, were you home and did you hear anything from Barry's house? Any noises?"

"Hmm...let me think." As he considered my question, he adjusted a pile of paperbacks, lining them up neatly. "Of course, I remember. Barry was on his deck in the evening, talking loudly on the phone. Then in the evening he was watching TV. It was one of those awful Jay Casanova action movies—" He cut himself off. "Sorry, Bernie, I didn't mean—"

"Jay's movies are junk. As long as you don't bad-mouth *Silver & Gold*, Phil, we're good. But tell me, what did you hear?"

"What didn't I hear? It felt like the movie was playing in my head. The gunshots and yelling were so loud, the noise kept me up half the night. Barry turned down the volume around 1 am, but only after I called him and gave him a piece of my mind."

My heart did a little cartwheel. "You talked to him? Was it on his landline?"

"I don't know his cell phone number, only his landline. He promised to keep it down, as he always did. This time, he turned down the volume right after our chat. Or maybe he put on headphones, so he could keep watching. Because he stayed up watching TV."

"How do you know?"

"I had a hard time getting back to sleep and stayed awake, reading a book for hours. At 3 am, I got a glass of water, and I could see the lights from the TV flickering against Barry's windows."

"Did you hear him again? Did you hear his front door slam or a car leave?"

Phil looked thoughtful. Then shook his head. "No, everything was quiet."

My heart was galloping, my whole body tingling with excitement. This was the crack in the case I'd been looking for—the one that might open the entire thing up. "So Barry's alibi had been a lie. He wasn't in New York City the night before Marty died. He was home alone, and nobody but you knew."

Phil still looked thoughtful. "Well, I suppose someone knew..."

"What do you mean?"

"Barry spoke on the phone in the evening. Then there was a call in the middle of the night. I don't know when—I didn't check the time—but it was after I called. His balcony door must have been ajar."

"What did you hear?"

"It sounded like a business call. 'He knows about the losses on his account,' he said. 'But I've told you, I'll fix it. Marty will back down and I'll plug the gap. No, we're not going to Plan B. Don't go and do anything stupid.'"

"Barry was never in New York City," I said when I found Nat and Angelica, the words tumbling out of me.

They sat on a park bench in Puccini Park, a perfect spot for observing the event. A crowd had gathered on the wide lawn, where rows of booths offered entertainment, souvenirs, and snacks. At the whack-a-mole and balloon darts, kids squealed and cheered each other on. On the bandstand in the very middle, local jazz musicians played renditions of classic Rat Pack songs. Mayor Blink stood on the bandstand, swaying along to the music.

I couldn't believe the killer was within sight.

Nat and Angelica turned from the entertainment, staring at me.

"Barry lied," I said, plonking down between them.

Angelica frowned, no doubt scandalized that someone would concoct a false alibi. Nat nodded, as if he'd expected as much.

"Something about Barry never added up," he said. "So, he was in Carmine the whole time?"

"He was at home the night the killer broke into Moroni's and planted the poisonous cookies." I waved the FBI folder, and couldn't help but grin triumphantly. "This file documents everything, and Phil Palladino has confirmed it. Not only was Barry's alibi a lie, he had a suspicious conversation with Mayor Blink in the middle of the night."

I summarized what Phil Palladino had told me, including what he'd overheard Barry say on the phone.

"It all makes sense. Barry had a motive to kill Marty. He'd been stealing from him, and Marty found out. But in fact, Barry meddled in much worse things—money laundering for the mob—and couldn't afford to stop now. He had a partner, who had dug himself into just as deep a hole, stealing and embezzling public funds."

I showed them the evidence in the FBI surveillance documents.

"Mayor Blink," Nat said. He looked thoughtful. "'Don't go and do anything stupid'—is that what Barry said on the phone?"

I nodded. "Now you see."

"See what?" someone said behind me. Chief Tedesco stood behind the park bench, her head cocked with interest.

The sun flashed off her sunglasses. "What do you have there, Bernie?"

"Uh," I mumbled, as I stuffed the contents back into the manila folder, except the photo of myself—my stubborn instinct told me to hang onto it. "It fell off a truck..."

"You'd better explain," she said, taking the folder from me and flipping through the sheets of paper. She let out a low whistle. "*Mamma mia...*"

I explained everything, leaving out how I had come by a folder full of FBI surveillance material. When I was done, Chief Tedesco pushed her sunglasses down on her nose and gave me a schoolmarmish look.

"This wouldn't have anything to do with Roberta LaRosa, would it?"

I shook my head and probably looked like I was vigorously shaking off a swarm of bees.

With a low harrumph, Chief Tedesco pushed up her sunglasses to the bridge of her nose. But she didn't press the matter, and I was quick to change the topic: "So, you see, Mayor Blink must have panicked. He thought Marty had discovered their embezzlements, and he'd blow the whistle. While Barry tried to clean up the mess, Blink was busy breaking into Moroni's and preparing poison to murder Marty before he could snitch."

Chief Tedesco, as she flipped through the pages, said, "I always thought that Barry's New York alibi, if it hadn't been for his sister corroborating it, sounded paper thin. So that makes sense. And the fact that he was going to tattle to the feds explains why he was murdered. The killer had wanted to silence him."

"Mayor Blink," I said, nodding. "Imagine how he must have reacted when the feds came after Barry. Somehow, Blink must have guessed or even discovered that his partner in crime would rat him out to the feds. So, he killed Barry, desperately trying to pin the murder on Angelica."

Chief Tedesco closed the manila folder. "It's a nice, tidy theory. There's only one problem."

"What?"

"At the beginning of this investigation, I looked into all the guests at Barry's garden party, in case the killer was among them. Mayor Blink has a solid alibi for the break-in. His wife and kids have corroborated it. Same for the night before the murder."

"And what about Barry's death?"

"The mayor was in a meeting with Deputy Mayor Palumbo."

My heart sank. "You mean we've got nothing?"

"Not nothing, Bernie." She slapped the folder. "Mayor Blink's guilty of embezzling public funds, and it's all documented here."

"But the murder..."

"The murder remains unsolved. But with this evidence, I've got enough to cuff the mayor right away." A big smile spread across Chief Tedesco's face. It was a rare thing to see her grin like this. "Oh, I'll enjoy cuffing this *disgraziad*."

14

From a distance, Nat, Angelica, and I watched Chief Tedesco, flanked by Officer Fontana, arrest Mayor Blink. It was like watching a silent film. First, the mayor waved his hands, jabbing a finger at the air in righteous indignation. Then, Chief Tedesco, with her thumbs stuck into her belt like a sheriff from the Old West, talked and talked, no doubt explaining how much damning evidence the police had. Blink's hands stilled and his arms fell to his sides. His shoulders slumped. Fontana cuffed him, and as Mayor Blink stumbled away from the festivities, he hung his head.

"What a sad end to his career," Angelica said. "What kind of person steals from his community?"

At the edge of the park stood a police cruiser. Officer Fontana put a hand on Mayor Blink's head and guided him into the back. Then closed the door.

Nat said, "We still don't know who killed Marty and Barry."

I sighed. No matter how close I'd felt to solving the case, no matter how much I wanted the evidence to point to these dirty guys—Barry Longo, Mayor Blink, not to mention Rick Alfano—I couldn't deny the facts: none of them could have killed Marty.

Chief Tedesco was thrilled. With the evidence from Roberta, she'd bagged a bad guy. One piece of FBI evidence remained: the photograph of me from Barry Longo's garden party. I stared at it, and stared, and stared, as if by straining my eyes I could coerce it to give up its hidden meaning. I sighed. Why would the photograph reveal anything now, when a whole heap of FBI surveillance information had provided no leads?

"Let it go." Angelica put a hand on my arm. "It's Italian Day. We should enjoy ourselves and forget this unpleasant business. How about joining me for some food and drinks, *mia cara*?"

As usual, she was worrying about me. She always worried about others first. And here I was, absorbed by my own thoughts. How painful must it be for her to attend the Italian Day Celebration, having to eat the food she herself should have been serving?

"Are you sure you want that?" I asked, folding up the photograph and stuffing it into the back pocket of my jeans.

"A person's got to eat. Besides, I'm curious to see how Betsy's catering tastes. It's one thing to provide food for a garden party, another to feed hundreds at a town celebration. Maybe we'll be pleasantly surprised."

At the end of Puccini Park's long lawn stood clusters of sycamore trees. Under their shade, the catering staff from Italian Dream had set up food stands. There was an assortment of classic Italian foods: sausages and peppers, lasagna, half a dozen kinds of pasta, including spaghetti with meatballs.

As we approached, I caught Anthony Ferrante multitasking: eating a sausage off a paper plate, stuffing it into his mouth, while trying to keep an eye on the crowd.

"Uh, hey, Bernie..." Grease from the sausage squirted down his uniform. "Aw, *maron'!*"

A couple of stands also offered baked goods, and my heart shrank to see grownups and kids gorge themselves on pignoli cookies and cannolis—which ought to have come from Moroni's.

Angelica led the way to the pasta stand. Italian Dream staff in white t-shirts with the company logo hustled to dish out penne arrabbiata, lasagna, and spaghetti with meatballs.

Lily, a baseball cap covering her shaved head, smiled at me. She glanced nervously at Angelica.

"Hi, Bernie. What can I get you?"

"I thought you'd be serving baked goods," I said.

"That's my passion, all right, but my boss is pretty strict about wanting to handle all the baking herself." Lily shrugged. "I guess that's her passion, too."

Angelica smiled at Lily. "If baking is your passion, you really should come to Moroni's one day and I can show you some tricks." She faltered. "When the bakery opens again, that is."

Lily's eyes widened. "Are you serious?"

"I'd never lie," Angelica said. "Certainly, not about baking."

I laughed. "That's the truth. By the way, Angelica, Lily has this notebook..."

I explained what Lily had told me about how she documented her recipes, and soon enough, she herself grew confident enough to talk about her study of baking. She grew even more excited as Angelica explained how she'd used the same techniques when she had studied under a master baker in Sicily.

Meanwhile, my mind drifted.

Notebook...

Somewhere, deep in the recesses of my brain, a pebble of an idea dropped into water. Ripples eddied outward. There was something important about what Lily had told me—something about the notebook—but what?

In the middle of Lily's excited talk about baking, she was interrupted. Betsy shuffled over to Lily. She was wearing an apron that said, "Italian Dream—the best food and baked goods you could imagine." Her eyes were bloodshot and red-rimmed. She looked pale and haggard, the picture of grief.

"You came, Angelica," she said, her voice catching on a sob.

"My sweet Betsy, of course I came. But why did you? You should be home, drinking tea, surrounded by family. What are you doing at work?"

"I can't afford to stay home, and besides, I've got no one. No family. Now that—now that—Barry is—Barry is—"

She broke down sobbing, and Angelica reached out, but her arms couldn't cover the distance of the deep table. Lily stared at her boss, and dug her hands into her pockets, looking anywhere but at the spectacle of Betsy weeping.

"You wouldn't believe me," Betsy said, directing the accusation at me. "I told you my brother was innocent. I told you he could never hurt anyone. But you wouldn't believe me. Nobody would. And now he's—"

She dug a tissue out of her pocket and blew her nose loudly.

"Sorry," she muttered.

She cleared her throat. She straightened her spine. In a steady, lifeless voice, she asked Lily to go help other customers and leave the serving to her.

"I can handle the bakery station?" Lily asked, a look of surprise and hope on her face.

"Go," Betsy grumbled and turned her attention to us. "Now, what can I get you to eat?"

Angelica ordered the penne, Nat the lasagna, and I got the spaghetti meatballs. We didn't speak. We waited for Betsy to dish up the food on paper plates. Her hands trembled as she served us, and when she got to my spaghetti meatballs, she fumbled the plate and spilled it. Sauce sloshed onto my jeans.

"Oh, no," she cried out. She grabbed a wad of napkins and held them out to me. "I am so sorry, Bernie."

"Don't worry about it."

I grabbed a bunch of napkins and dabbed at my pants, and Angelica and Nat helped, too. By the time I had gotten the worst off, Betsy stood ready with a fresh plate of spaghetti meatballs.

"Enjoy," she said, smiling.

We walked away with a worried glance at each other.

"She's in a bad place," Angelica said. "Poor woman."

Not far from the food stations stood a park bench and a garbage can. A young couple sat on the bench, so Angelica, Nat, and I found a spot on the lawn in front of it.

Balancing the plate of food on my knees, I glanced over my shoulder and caught Betsy staring at me. The yellowing leaves of the sycamore framed her, and a memory stirred in the depths of my mind. I shook my head. The solution to the murder was close. So why couldn't I see it yet?

Angelica speared a piece of penne and chewed it. "Not bad. Although—and I'm clearly biased—it's nothing like Carlo's."

Nat tasted his lasagna and agreed. "Decent. Good, but not great. How are the meatballs, Bernie?"

I cut a meatball in half and jabbed it with my fork. That memory was still niggling the back of my brain, demanding my attention. There was something about that photo. And Lily's notebook.

I put down my fork. "You know, somehow, I feel I got the wrong end of this case from the beginning. First, I thought Marty was killed because of money. *Sequere pecuniam* was his favorite Latin phrase. Well, I followed the money. Rick wanted it. Barry stole it. It seemed every greedy guy had a reason to kill Marty. But what if the money was a wild goose chase...?"

My musing shattered, interrupted by a cry. The young man and woman in front of us howled as they jumped up on the park bench. A rat darted out from under a bush, weaving in and out of the bench's iron legs.

Angelica, Nat, and I got to our feet, too.

The rat scurried away and rounded the nearby garbage can, vanishing again.

"Did I get it?" Peter jumped onto the path, holding his camera to his face. "Did I get it?"

He lowered the camera and fiddled with it, apparently looking through the photos he'd taken.

He let out a groan. "It's a blur...you can't even see what it is."

"Don't worry, Peter," Nat said. "I have a feeling there are many more rats where that one came from. Plus, you got a shot of Mayor Blink, didn't you?"

"Mayor Blink?" Peter looked confused. "What about him?"

"Oh, no." We all looked at each other, and Nat gave Peter a sympathetic look. "Chief Tedesco arrested him on suspicion of stealing public funds."

"I can't believe what bad luck I'm having," Peter said,

sounding miserable. "Every story seems to be one step ahead of me. I'm always halfway across town when something interesting happens."

He stalked off, glaring at the bushes, his hand gripping the camera.

I rarely saw eye to eye with Peter, but right now, he got my sympathy. After all, he'd been the one to raise a red flag when he'd noticed Mayor Blink's irregularities. He'd caught the first signs, and ought to have been rewarded with a good snapshot of the mayor's disgraceful exit. If he persisted, I hoped he'd get a good shot of a rat.

Snapshot...

Wait a minute. I dug the photo out of my pocket and unfolded it. I went to the park bench, now unoccupied, and laid the photo down, smoothing out its creases.

"What are you looking for?" Nat asked me, joining me on one side. Angelica stood on the other.

All three of us stared at the photo for a while.

There was Barry, sipping his cocktail; Mayor Blink, lobster roll in hand, scowling at his partner in crime; Marty, whose lack of interest in Crystal was glaringly obvious; and me, staring off at the crowd. And somehow, I was the center of the photo, the most significant thing.

Or was I?

No. I'd been wrong. None of the central characters were significant.

"The purple flowers," I mumbled. "And the face..."

I picked up the photo, studying it closely again. I'd been looking for the answer in the foreground, and now saw that the camera had captured the wrong thing. The blurry background turned the wall of flowers into a swirl of colors, nearly swallowing the one person who wasn't in focus.

Purple flowers, I thought. *Pretty purple flowers.* Then

recalled what Lily had said when she'd shown me her notebook: *At work, we have a food dehydrator, but my boss doesn't let me use it.*

Suddenly, all the pieces of the puzzle came together. I let out a long sigh of relief. Finally, I understood.

"Of course," I said. "Barry lied about his alibi..."

"Uh, Bernie," Nat said.

"Yeah?"

"Don't eat the meatballs."

I turned. The rat, apparently seizing the opportunity while I was busy studying the photo, had darted out to munch on my food. It lay next to my plate, as lifeless as a doll.

Nat and I looked at each other.

We both spoke the only word that mattered: "Poison."

A GIRL SCREAMED. A man cursed loudly. A woman said, "Hey, watch your mouth—there are kids here." Then she saw the rat, too, and fired off a volley of obscene Italian swear words, grabbed her kids, and ushered them away.

Officer Anthony Ferrante came running, still chewing his sausage.

"What happened? What happened?"

Meanwhile, Peter gleefully photographed the pandemonium: click, click, click.

I whipped around. Across the lawn, by the food stations, Betsy Longo tore off her apron. She flung it aside and bolted. Lily, standing in her way, nearly got knocked down when Betsy shouldered past her. She emerged from the food stations in a run.

"Stop her," I yelled.

Angelica and Nat followed my gaze.

Anthony was busy lifting the dead rat with a napkin and putting it into a cardboard box by the garbage can. He glanced around at me, confused. "Stop who?"

To escape the park, Betsy could either double back and head for Old Lake Road or go straight. She was heading straight. Soon she'd reach the back alleys behind Garibaldi Avenue, then Garibaldi itself. Which way would she go?

I could block one exit but not both.

Barreling toward her escape, Betsy nearly tripped over a man's dog, leaping over it, and she threw a harried look back at me.

Then she hit the sidewalk. Another 20 feet and she'd vanish into the alley.

If only I had a way of blocking that alley. Then I could stand guard down the street and ensure she didn't make it to Garibaldi.

Looking down at the ground, I caught sight of the cardboard box with the dead rat, and it gave me an idea.

I picked up the box, doing my absolute best not to look inside. Of course, I couldn't not look.

Ugh.

Forget what it is. It's like one of those cat toys—rubber, not real.

I swallowed, refusing to get queasy.

Then I bolted, sprinting out of the park and off the curb and into the street that ringed the block. But Betsy had a head start. In only a few strides, she'd vanish down the alley. Then she could run behind the Garibaldi Avenue stores, from Milano Books down to Moroni's, and slip through the maze of neighborhood streets that lay behind.

I gripped the box firmly, swung it, and let go.

It flew a few yards and then hit the ground with a thunk,

sliding across the sidewalk. It came to a standstill right where I'd aimed: at the mouth of the alley.

Just as Betsy reached it.

She was about to jump over the box, like she'd jumped over that man's dog, but then she saw it. She saw the box wasn't empty.

She stopped as abruptly as if she'd hit a wall, her body going rigid, and she screamed.

"Rat!"

She screamed. And screamed. And screamed.

15

"This is the best Italian Day we've ever celebrated," Rose Calabrese rasped.

Sofa Ruggiero agreed. "The entertainment has been something else, but the food is the real highlight."

She didn't mean my poisoned meatballs.

We were standing on Garibaldi Avenue, the main street having been hastily shut down. Police barriers blocked either end, and it seemed the whole town thronged around the entrances to Carlo's and Moroni's.

The front doors of the restaurant and the bakery stood wide open. Carlo had set up a table in front of his establishment, Angelica in front of hers, and while Maria handled savory orders, I managed the sweet ones.

Miraculously, despite the long lines, everyone was on good behavior. No one jostled their neighbors or yelled about the waiting time. There was a buzz, an excitement, even joy that ran through the crowd, and despite the disastrous turn of the events, Carmine felt more festive than ever.

I handed Sofia and Rose the cannolis and coffees they'd ordered and turned to the next person in line.

Peter Piatek passed us, snapping photos of the crowd, a grin on his face.

"Bernie, I'm getting one wonderful photo after another," he told me, almost having to yell over the din of talking. "And I just published two fresh news stories. Did you get the breaking news alert on your phone?"

"I did, Peter. But honestly, 'Mayor Rat'? And the 'Killer Caterer'? You've got to work on your monikers."

He only laughed. "They're silly, right? But unforgettable. Readership is skyrocketing."

He hurried off, clearly giddy and eager to take more photos. I couldn't help but smile. Peter never stopped moving, never stopped trying to get a good story for *The Carmine Enquirer*.

"What a party," Nat said, emerging from the bakery with another tray of cookies. He'd offered to lend a helping hand, and boy, was I glad he did. In front of me was a sea of happy, hungry faces. Angelica came out with a tray, too, and together, we all three replenished the Tupperware containers we kept the cookies in. I had taped labels to each one, indicating the contents: pignoli, pizzelle, cuccidati, and so on. Next to them stood three coffee urns and stacks of cups.

Angelica said, "With all the excitement, I still haven't quite worked out how you realized Betsy was the killer. Well, apart from the obvious attempt to kill you."

I dug the photo from the garden party out of my pocket. "Look, purple flowers. It's too blurry to see in the photo, but I remember them from the garden party, and from when I visited Barry afterward. They're bell-like flowers. You could also describe them as hood-like."

"Monkshood," Angelica said, and put a hand to her mouth in shock.

"That's right. Monkshood. Wolfsbane. Barry had the deadly flowers in his garden. The murder weapon is right here in the photo. And so is the killer."

I pointed at the killer in the photo, almost as blurred out as the flowers.

Angelica and Nat exchanged looks.

"That's Betsy," I said. "Whoever poisoned Marty stole Angelica's notebook to replicate his favorite cookies. That meant the killer had to bake the cookies, and do it well enough that Angelica didn't notice they'd been swapped. The killer also had to know how to add crushed wolfsbane to the ingredients—not an easy thing to get your hands on. But I remembered something Lily told me—that her boss had a dehydrator at work and that baking was her passion. Well, our killer had to be a baker. Which also explains why Betsy knew about Marty's favorite cookie. Surely, a financial adviser or the mayor wouldn't casually ask what Marty's favorite cookie was, nor consider it as a murder weapon. A baker would, though. Especially if that baker was having an affair with the victim." I shook my head, still amazed at how far off track I'd gotten. "All along, I had the motive wrong. It wasn't about money; it was about love. At the garden party, I overheard Marty talk to someone. 'I said all there is to say—don't push me.' Marty had an affair. Crystal found out, and he broke it off. That day at Barry Longo's, Marty told Betsy once and for all that it was over."

"But she broke into the bakery *before* the garden party," Nat said.

"Yes, he'd ended it earlier, and she'd already planned her revenge. But maybe she hoped he'd change his mind last minute. He didn't."

A kid ordered a bagful of all the cookies, a half dozen of

each kind, and I got his order ready as Nat, Angelica, and I continued to talk.

"So, Marty dismissed her," Nat said, "and she carried out her plan."

"Right. She'd broken into Moroni's to steal the keys and the notebook. Her plan was to kill Marty the following weekend. But she needed an alibi. Hanging around her brother's parties, she must have guessed he was up to his neck in illegal activities. So, she pressed her brother into providing it, threatening to spill his dirty secrets, if he didn't cooperate."

"We were so focused on Barry's alibi," Nat said, "we forgot it was also *her* alibi."

I nodded. "When she guessed that Barry was going to hand her over to the Feds to get a lenient sentence, she chose to kill him in a desperate attempt to protect herself. Once again, she tried to pin the murder on Angelica."

"But why me?" Angelica asked.

"Jealousy," I said with a shrug, guessing. "You had Marty once. You have a successful bakery. But it was also convenient. She needed a patsy, and the ex-wife is as likely a suspect as the spurned lover."

"How does Mayor Blink fit in?" Nat asked.

"He was Barry's partner in crime. But far less accomplished. He got nervous and sloppy, and kept calling Barry to anxiously suggest they pull the plug."

"Plan B," Nat said. "But Barry didn't budge."

"Exactly. Betsy knew about the mayor's involvement, too, and immediately after killing her brother, she blackmailed the mayor into giving her the contract to cater the Italian Day Celebration. A greedy move. But desperate, especially now that his partner in crime was dead, Mayor Blink agreed and yanked the job from Carlo's and Moroni's, claiming it was because of bad PR."

"That rat," Angelica said, an unusually forceful accusation coming from her.

A man waiting in line visibly flinched at the mention of a rat, and he looked around nervously.

"You didn't see a rat, did you?"

Angelica assured him that Garibaldi Avenue was entirely rat free.

"The only thing you have to worry about," she said with a smile, "is eating too many of my pignoli cookies."

She headed back inside to make more cookies.

"I can't believe it was only an hour ago we were all in Puccini Park," Nat said, looking at his watch.

After the mayor's arrest, and the incident with the rat, Chief Tedesco had contacted the Sanitation Department, who'd sent a crew to the park. People hardly noticed them. Everyone was busy gaping in wonder at Betsy Longo being arrested. When Anthony cuffed her and led her away, her face was awash with tears, her lips moving as she mumbled incoherently. Just then, the sanitation inspector announced that, because of vermin, the party had to be shut down. A groan swept through the park, but Chief Tedesco came to the rescue. She'd gotten up on a park bench and whistled loudly—with thumb and index finger in her mouth to amplify the sound—and when the park had gone quiet, she made an announcement of her own: Garibaldi Avenue would be shut down and the party would continue. A collective cheer had risen from the crowd.

"I have a feeling Chief Tedesco's popularity will shoot up after this," I said.

"If we can feed the crowd enough cookies to keep them happy," he said.

He hurried back inside to get a fresh tray as I bagged another handful of cookies for a family.

"A cannoli, please, and a coffee," a woman in a baseball cap and dark sunglasses said. She'd pulled the cap way down over her face. Still, there was no mistaking the voice.

"Hi, Roberta."

She gave me a nod and glanced to the left and the right, making sure no one was watching us—only people eagerly waiting their turn to order cannolis or pignoli cookies.

I held a cup under one of the coffee urns, filling it. "Want sugar in that coffee?"

She shook her head. "Black. I'm off sugar again. Mayor Blink is in custody, so is Betsy Longo. Both mysteries have been solved. Plus, the Feds raided Barry's home and came up with a treasure trove of evidence, including files that will help investigations into one of New Jersey's biggest crime families."

I handed her a paper plate with a cannoli and a steaming cup of coffee. She bent the paper plate around the cannoli, the way you would have a slice of pizza, so she could hold it in one hand, the coffee in the other.

I studied her. This woman had stood by my side during the Jay Casanova trial and my time in witness protection. Even now, when I was no longer the responsibility of the U.S. Marshalls Service, she continued to lend me a hand.

"Roberta, why do you spend time watching Carmine?"

She froze, mid-bite. After a pause, she bit down and chewed her cannoli. Then swallowed. She washed it down with coffee.

"I'll tell you," she said, and I leaned forward, eager to clear up this mystery. She quirked a smile. "Someday."

"Roberta..."

"Thanks for the coffee and cannoli."

She turned and slipped into the crowd, her baseball cap bobbing along and then vanishing into the sea of people. I let out a sigh. Roberta was a mystery. Would I someday solve the puzzle and understand why, even after I'd left witness protection, she took such an interest in what happened to me in Carmine?

I got busy serving the next customer, and then the next.

The third turned out to be Chief Tedesco.

I gave her a big smile. "You're the hero of the day for saving the celebration."

"And opening my bakery again," Angelica said, coming out of the bakery with a tray of cannolis.

"Maybe you'll like me even more when you see what I've brought you," Chief Tedesco said, and held out an object.

Angelica's eyes widened, and she nearly dropped the tray of cannolis. "My notebook!"

After putting down the tray, she accepted the notebook from Chief Tedesco and opened it, flipping through the pages. She let out a sigh. "It's all here. Nothing's damaged. How did you get it?"

"As soon as Betsy Longo was arrested, we searched her home. We found your notebook as well as a stash of ground aconitine."

There was an ear-deafening screech and a thump that rattled the windows. We turned to see what the noise was.

"It's the band," Chief Tedesco explained. "They're setting up to play."

"Without a stage?"

"They're making do with what's available."

I craned my neck and saw, across Garibaldi, that people were moving around on the rooftop of Parisi & Parisi. The band was planning to play from up there. Chief Tedesco explained that Gino Parisi reinforced the building to carry extra weight for a rooftop garden, which he'd never gotten around to installing.

"Is it safe?" I asked.

"Absolutely."

There was another screech and thump, and then the twang of a guitar. Something on the roof fell over and clattered.

"Even so, I'd better go make sure they don't do anything stupid," she said and wandered off.

"She's a good person," Angelica said, hugging the notebook to her chest.

"You say that about everyone."

"Well, then, Chief Tedesco is a great person."

She looked so genuinely happy, so entirely herself for the first time in ages, that it filled me with warmth. The nightmare was behind us, and now we could focus on getting Moroni's back on track. We could focus on crispy pizzelles, chewy pignoli cookies, and mouth-watering cannolis.

I turned to the next customer. "What would you like?"

And an electric shock jolted me.

In front of me stood the mysterious man I'd caught snooping outside Moroni's a few days ago. He was wearing the same ludicrous getup: a floppy fisherman's hat, a large pair of sunglasses, and a trench coat.

"I'd like to speak with the owner," he demanded.

"I'm the owner," Angelica said. "I'm Angelica Moroni."

The man stared at her for a moment. Then he looked right and then left, just as Roberta had, careful in case someone was watching. He tugged at his sunglasses, pulling them off. Beneath them, he had large, gentle eyes. He smiled with what seemed like a hint of shyness.

He held out his right hand.

"The name's George," he said. "George Pullman."

I heard a gasp behind me. Nat stood in the doorway, his eyes as wide as espresso cups.

"*The* George Pullman?" he whispered. "The famous food critic?"

George Pullman nodded, giving another glance to his right and then his left.

"Sadly, I have to hide my identity. Otherwise, I get preferential treatment wherever I go."

Something clicked in my mind, another piece of the puzzle coming together.

"You were eating lunch when Jacky Yu was at Carlo's, weren't you? You were the professor eating linguini."

He smiled. "Another disguise. And let me tell you, Carlo's has the best linguini with clam sauce I've ever had. Thanks to my disguise, I could eat it in peace, even while you were pestering Jacky."

I felt the heat rise to my face. "I did pester her, didn't I?"

"Only a little. Anyway, she's going to write a glowing review of Carlo's. But I tell you, bad luck deprived her of a truly sublime experience when she wasn't able to visit Moroni's."

He gave a little bow to Angelica.

Angelica beamed. "I'm so glad you like my baked goods."

"Like them? I've stopped by the bakery before. Unfortunately, you were closed. But today, I bribed a kid to buy a selection of all your cookies, so I could eat them in peace. And they're spectacular. I'm going to write a review about the magnificent culinary duo of Carmine, New Jersey— Carlo and Angelica—whose savory and sweet flavors truly make the angels sing. I can't wait to come back when Moroni's is open for normal business."

"Oh, please do," Angelica said. "And I hope you'll feel free to come as yourself."

"I might," George said. Then winked. "Or you might never know I was here."

He grabbed another bag of cookies to go and headed off, sunglasses back on, so he could move incognito through the crowd.

Angelica, Nat, and I watched him go. I couldn't keep from grinning. With George's glowing review, Moroni's was more than back in business. We'd soon be booming. But what mattered the most was that Angelica was back home in her bakery. Everyone was happy again.

I munched on a pignoli cookie. I sipped some coffee.

The lead singer of the band, their equipment finally up and running on the rooftop, counted "1, 2, 3, 4..." and they launched into a rendition of the song "Volare," one of my favorites.

I wasn't the only one who loved it.

Everywhere on Garibaldi Avenue, couples grabbed each other and swung to the music. Kids mimicked the adults. Someone called out, "Hey, Little Angelo, that's the way to do it." People laughed.

Soon, all the people of Carmine—and the visitors who'd come to celebrate Italian Day—were dancing in the street.

THANK you so much for visiting Carmine. Join Bernie and her friends for another culinary cozy mystery in book 4:

Meatballs, Mafia, and Murder

Oh, and want a FREE short story? Sign up for my

newsletter updates on new books and I'll send the free story to you by email:

https://mpblackbooks.com/newsletter/

Finally, if you enjoyed this book, please take a moment to leave a review online. It makes it easier for other readers to find the book. Thanks so much!

Turn the page to read chapter 1 of *Meatballs, Mafia, and Murder* (Book 4)...

16

MEATBALLS, MAFIA, AND MURDER EXCERPT

"Frankie Fazio shot Vinnie Albanese three times. Between the silencer on his gun and the neighbor's thumping music, nobody heard. Frankie left the rival mobster on the bed. Vinnie, for once, looked peaceful. On his way out of the apartment, Frankie caught sight of the pot on the stove and stopped. He lifted the lid and raised the wooden spoon to his mouth. He winced. 'Vinnie, you *stunad*, why'd you go and use those cheap tomatoes? You ruined the sauce.'"

Marco Puglisi, bestselling author of the Frankie F. mafia thrillers, closed his latest book.

The audience at Milano Books, which had been so quiet during the reading that you could've heard a pin drop, burst into enthusiastic applause.

Puglisi, a tiny man with giant glasses, smiled. His teeth were large, too, which made his face look donkey-like. If donkeys wore bifocals. His glasses kept slipping, and he pushed them up to the bridge of his nose as he thanked the audience.

On the table in front of Peewee sat a stack of hardbacks.

One copy rested against a book stand, revealing the dark, gritty cover and the bold title: *Sicilians Wear Black*.

I leaned close to Angelica, keeping my voice low.

"His books seem so..." I looked for the right word. "*Muscular*. I expected a tough guy. But Puglisi's nothing like the mobsters he writes about."

"Everyone calls him 'Peewee,'" she said. "Ever since he was a kid, he's been called that. Even when he taught English at Carmine High. And no amount of fame will change that."

Looking over at Peewee Puglisi, I caught sight of Phil Palladino, who sat next to him. Phil owned Milano Books, the only bookstore in Carmine, New Jersey, and he'd been so nervous in the days before this big Saturday night event that he must've bought every antacid on the shelf at Martini's Italian Market.

Now he gave me a big smile and a thumbs up. That made me happy. I knew how much tonight meant to him. Plus, it was good exposure for all of Carmine's businesses.

Peewee, a Carmine native, had gained national fame with his hard-boiled tales of a mafia hitman, and in addition to attracting many locals, the event had brought journalists and readers from New York City. Milano Books was packed.

There was the kind of buzz tonight you might expect at a Christmas party. I imagined book events in the city were more formal, more muted. But this was an excuse for Carmine to celebrate one of its own, showcasing that even our little town could produce a bestselling author.

Phil adjusted his cardigan and got to his feet. After giving profuse thanks to the author by his side, he said, "Mr. Puglisi will sign your books now, so please line up."

People got up from the rows of chairs facing Peewee's table. Over the din of chairs scraping and people talking,

Phil raised his voice: "Oh, and if you want nibbles and drinks, our speakeasy is open."

He chuckled as he gestured toward Angelica and me.

Our food station, a couple of paces from Peewee's table, had a sign that said, "Moroni's Speakeasy." We both wore black shirts with white ties, white suspenders, and pin-striped pants in a nod to 1920s mafia outfits. It didn't matter that Peewee's books had a more contemporary setting—the guests got a kick out of the costumes.

"I wore a costume just like that last Halloween," Sofia Ruggiero told me.

"Costume?" her friend, Rose Calabrese said, a mischievous glint in her eye. "Those were clothes from your youth."

Sofia swatted her friend, and together, they cackled at the joke. The two ladies, both soon to be celebrating their 80th birthday, never failed to put a smile on my face.

"Angelica," Rose said, studying the food on display. "You've outdone yourself again."

She was right, of course. At a typical book reading, guests would be lucky to get a glass of tepid tap water and a few stale pretzel sticks. But Angelica, owner of Moroni's Italian Bakery, and also my boss and friend, had prepared an enticing spread.

There was a platter with *bruschetta*, made with Angelica's own fresh-baked bread and topped with fresh, chopped tomatoes and basil. She'd made tiny pastry puffs stuffed with ricotta and roasted red peppers, nicely complemented by miniature meatballs on skewers, courtesy of her brother, Carlo, who owned Carmine's best restaurant. A cheese platter with a variety of hard cheeses offered easily held finger food. And guests could choose from several non-alcoholic drinks: a sparkling lemonade with ginger; a pitcher of lemon, mint, and cucumber-infused water; and a red drink

—a raspberry spritzer—which Angelica had dubbed a "Carmine Bloody Mary."

While Angelica and I were busy serving food and drinks to guests, my friend Nat Natale was also busy. As an employee of the public library and Carmine historical society, he'd had the clever idea of setting up a table with "mafia artifacts." He and his boss, Mrs. Viola, explained the history of the objects to anyone interested. Many were. The table stood near the checkout counter, and it had drawn as many people as our "speakeasy" station.

An hour or so later, the line for the book signing grew shorter and the crowd at our food station thinned out. Angelica put together a plate with bruschetta, meatballs, and the ricotta puffs, and handed it to me.

"Bernie, *mia cara*, why don't you take this over to Nat and Mrs. Viola? We don't want them to go hungry."

I smiled.

Angelica was a beautiful person. On the inside and the outside. Chocolate-brown eyes. Black hair with a single white streak, caught up in a complex architecture of hairpins. And a smile that could melt an ice cube's heart.

Her greatest worry in life seemed to be that people wouldn't get their fair share of Italian food.

"Go," she said. "Go."

So I went. And I was halfway across the room, thinking of what the world would look like if we didn't have people like Angelica, when I stopped dead.

Startled, and nearly dropping the plate of appetizers, I stared across the room.

By the bookstore entrance, leaning against the doorframe, was a person I knew well. She wore a baseball cap, pulled down low over her eyes. Yet I had no doubt: it was U.S. Marshall Roberta LaRosa.

It was thanks to Roberta that I'd landed in Carmine, New Jersey. Before my current life as Bernie Smyth, assistant baker and barista at Moroni's Italian Bakery, I had been the famous actress Bernadette Kovac. I starred as Eve Silver in America's favorite detective show on TV, *Silver & Gold*. That had all ended when I testified against my co-star, Jay Casanova, in his drug- and arms-trafficking trial, and had to go into witness protection.

Roberta had placed me in Carmine, and once the threat to my life passed, I'd chosen to stay in this wonderful town, even holding on to the identity Roberta had given me: goodbye, actress Bernadette Kovac—hello, Bernie Smyth, barista and assistant baker!

But since I'd left witness protection, Roberta and I didn't officially have anything to do with each other anymore. Still, she'd appeared in Carmine before. And that had been a sign of trouble.

I changed direction and headed toward her.

She was staring across the room, intent on someone else. Glancing over my shoulder, I tried to guess who she was so interested in. Was it someone in line to have their book signed? Or someone near the food station?

I turned my attention back to Roberta. But the space by the doorframe was empty.

Roberta had vanished.

OUTSIDE THE BOOKSTORE WINDOWS, the streetlights along Garibaldi Avenue, Carmine's main street, glowed softly in the dark evening. Rain sparkled in the light and ran down the glass. And as I gazed out, a USPS truck rumbled past.

For as long as I'd known Roberta, she'd moved around

incognito in a USPS truck, making "deliveries" at the most unexpected times.

I sighed. Whatever Roberta was up to, I hoped it wouldn't interfere with tonight's event. There'd been enough crime and murder in Carmine lately, and each time I'd been pulled into the investigation. For once, I wanted to stick to being Angelica's assistant.

I headed for the historical society's table.

Nat's fair hair fell over his round, steel-rimmed glasses. He swept his bangs aside and smiled. He was thrilled to see me—and not just because I'd brought provisions.

"Hey, Bernie, did you see what we put together for our display?"

I wasn't the only person craning forward to take a closer look. The display was a hit. And no wonder—because in addition to black-and-white photos of Carmine's early days, plus snapshots of "Carmine's most famous killers and crooks," the display included several intriguing items from Carmine's less cozy past: a Tommy gun, one of those classic gangster submachine guns with the distinctive drum magazine; a police helmet and billy club; a garrote wire for strangling; a hatchet, which I feared had not been used to chop wood; and a switchblade called the Italian stiletto.

"Don't worry," Nat said, as I handed him the plate with food. "The barrel of the Tommy gun's blocked and the Italian stiletto's a prop from a Broadway show. It couldn't cut butter on a hot summer's day."

The hatchet looked sharp, though. And I reached out to touch the blade.

"No touching," Mrs. Viola snapped, and I pulled back my hand, as if burned.

Mrs. Viola, Head Curator of the Carmine Historical Appreciation & Preservation Society, looked as stiff as one of

Madame Tussaud's wax figures. She stood a few feet behind the table, her arms crossed, and eyed everyone approaching the table with a suspicious glare.

Near her stood two people I didn't know, speaking in low voices. The woman had red hair cut into a severe bob, and her mouth curved downward in a frown. She held a briefcase in one hand. The burly man next to her reminded me of a missionary. If that missionary lifted a lot of weights. Guess it was his buzz cut, formal jacket, and white button-down shirt with a drab tie, everything so neatly pressed and buttoned up that he looked ready for church.

"These objects are great," I said to Nat and Mrs. Viola, while actually thinking what a nightmare this was.

Roberta LaRosa appears and disappears, and now there's a table-full of murder weapons? Mamma mia.

The flash from a camera went off next to me, and it made me jump. I turned to see Peter Piatek snapping photos of the display. Peter and I knew each other well. He ran *The Carmine Enquirer*, an online news site, and he had a passion for getting clicks on articles.

"We should get a shot of Marco Puglisi holding the Tommy gun."

"Over my dead body," the red-headed woman said.

Peter smiled. "You must be Anne Adams, Puglisi's agent."

"Agent, promoter, publicist, you name it, I do it all."

"Almost all," the big man next to her said.

She shrugged. "Nino here is Mr. Puglisi's so-called research assistant."

"If you don't like the Tommy gun," Peter said to Anne, "how about the hatchet?"

"A gun with a silencer—that's the only prop that makes sense. Have you even read the Frankie F. books?"

Nino put a hand on her arm and whispered, "Easy, Anne."

But Peter, apparently seeing an opportunity to talk to the author himself, had lost interest and moved on.

"Don't patronize me, Nino." Anne shook off his arm, and looked around at the bookstore with a sour expression on her face. "I can't believe I'm back in Carmine. I vowed never to set foot in this dump again. But the great Marco Puglisi, in spite of his unrivaled writing talent, can't pull himself away from this Podunk town."

"What's eating you, Anne?"

She didn't answer him. Instead, she strode across the room toward Peewee, who was still signing books. Nino set his jaw and trudged after her.

I was torn. I should head straight back to Angelica and help her, but even as I was telling myself that, my feet turned toward Anne and Nino. I took a step in their direction. Then stopped. Took a step toward Angelica, and stopped.

Nat laughed and leaned toward me. "Go ahead, Bernie. You know your curiosity will always win."

I groaned. "You can read me like an open book."

"Hey, I spend a lot of time at the public library—my reading skills are excellent." He winked at me. "Besides, I've seen you do this before. Go ahead. Snoop around a little. It won't kill you."

"Angelica needs me."

"Angelica's fine," he said. "Go."

With Nat's blessing, I allowed myself to take a detour.

After this, I'll head straight back to Angelica and help with the appetizers and drinks. Promise.

Peewee signed another book with a flourish and pushed his glasses up his nose.

Next, a man and a woman stepped forward. The woman had dark hair and a tentative smile, and she was the one who clutched one of Peewee's books.

Peewee cocked his head. "Don't I know you?"

She shook her head.

"We're visiting family," the man said, answering the question. "I went to Carmine High and actually took your English class. You can inscribe the book to me, Roberto Rizzoli."

"Roberto Rizzoli? Of course, now I recognize you. You're Anne's—"

"Ex," Anne cut in.

She stepped closer to the table.

Roberto greeted her with a nod.

"Anne," he said.

"Roberto," she said. "Did you come to gloat?"

"We came to make peace."

"We? Oh, you mean you and your little *lady*?" Only she didn't use the word lady. She used a very un-ladylike word for lady. "What, breaking up my marriage wasn't enough? Did you tell your friends about how you met this woman on one of your business trips?"

"You know that's not what happened..." Roberto sighed. "Let's forget it. We're visiting my mother and I asked Gina to come with me. That's all."

Just then, Phil interrupted with an announcement. The book signing was officially ending and Milano Books would be closing. There was much hubbub as guests said their goodbyes to Peewee and Phil, many thanking Angelica as well, and people streamed out into the street. Phil reminded Peewee that he'd arranged drinks and food for private guests after the bookstore closed. As the last people left the store, Roberto reached out and put a hand on Anne's arm and said, "Anne, we need to go."

"Stick around for the party, Rob. I'd love to get a chance to talk to your lovely wife."

She gave Gina a smile that would've made a cobra proud. Gina recoiled.

"That's generous of you, Anne," Roberto said, either unaware or willfully ignoring what had obviously been more of a threat than an invitation. "I hope we can put our past behind us. As you know, 'Blessed are the peacemakers, for they will be called the children of God.'"

Anne laughed. There was no joy in her laugh. "Your stupid piety doesn't fool me, Rob. I know the real you. If you could strangle me, you would."

At that very moment, there was a loud snick-snick, and I turned toward the entrance. Phil had locked the front door.

SUPPOSEDLY, the after-party was a more intimate affair. But Phil's idea of intimate was expansive. Us "crew members," so to speak, consisted of Peewee, Nino (Clemenza, I learned, was his last name), Anne, Phil, Mrs. Viola, Angelica, Nat, and me. Apart from Roberto and his wife, Gina, the other two dozen guests or so were editors, journalists, even a few fellow thriller writers, all connected to the publishing scene in New York City.

Angelica uncorked bottles of wine. People ate more ricotta puffs and meatballs and bruschetta, and they perched on chairs or leaned against bookshelves as they talked. Speakers mounted near the ceiling played music, Louis Prima wishing his signorina a *buona sera.* The noise level increased.

Angelica asked me to get more paper plates and cups from the office.

"Oh, and while you're out there," Phil called after me, "can you grab more wine as well, please?"

At the far end of the bookstore were two doors right next to each other—the restroom to the left and the back-room office to the right.

The door was ajar. As I pushed it open, I heard voices, and stopped. It was Peewee and Nino. I could just make out Nino's back from where I stood. Beyond him, a couch was pushed against a wall and to the left of that stood one of the shelves with book inventory.

"She's laying into that vino like there ain't no tomorrow," Peewee, out of sight, was saying. "And her breath reeked of booze when she showed up."

"Everyone has bad days, boss."

"The other day she was like this, too. And then there's the business of her arranging meetings behind my back."

"That was a mistake. I canceled it."

Behind me, I heard Nat call out, "Phil said you might need my help."

I was sure Nino and Peewee had heard him, so I said, "Great," and pushed the door wide open and walked in.

"Oh, hi," I said casually.

As Nat and I headed for the boxes of wine bottles Phil had left next to the inventory shelves at the back, Nino and Peewee headed for the door. Peewee gave me an apologetic smile and said, with a sigh, "Business stuff."

"I understand."

When Nat and I came out of the office, each with a box of wine and paper plates and cups balanced on top, Nino and Peewee had glasses of wine and were talking to guests.

On the surface, everything seemed fine. But my hands tingled. My nose itched, and I wrinkled it.

It was like smelling mold where I couldn't see it—something wasn't right.

I unboxed the bottles of wine and helped Angelica uncork another three bottles. Half a dozen bottles already stood empty on the table, and it seemed Anne was doing her best to polish another off. She jerked back her head, draining her wine glass. Then refilled it at once.

Gina came to the table, and I poured her a glass of wine.

"It's a beautiful bookshop," she said to me, seeming eager to talk.

"Are you a big reader?" I asked.

"Yes, but not thrillers. Not books like Marco Puglisi's."

"Too violent?"

She nodded and explained that she preferred books that focused on making the world a better place. As she talked, I caught sight of Mrs. Viola across the room, glaring at us.

Now, why is she looking at us as if we stole her favorite book?

A lot of her personal favorites were spiritual books, Gina was telling me.

"But I'll read anything that will bring more kindness into this world. There's been enough murder and pain—what the world needs is more love."

Anne snorted. She'd been eavesdropping.

"Talk about rose-tinted glasses."

She stumbled toward Gina, knocking into her with the briefcase and sloshing wine down her dress. Even as Gina dabbed her dress with napkins, Anne leaned close and whispered something.

I couldn't make out what it was, but it sounded a lot like, "He'll cheat again."

Whatever it was, the intention was clearly to upset Gina.

And it worked. Gina, who'd seemed high-strung from the moment I met her, set down her glass, nearly knocking it over, and spun around to flee.

Roberto caught her in his arms. Over Gina's head, he glared at Anne.

"You've got a lot of nerve..." he muttered through clenched teeth.

Anne stared at him. There was a long, icy silence.

Which was broken when Phil, Peewee, and Nino strolled over to the drinks table.

"So, years ago, you had an idea for a book, Nino. Remember that? You still think of writing it?"

Nino shook his head. "Nah. Too busy with my work for Mr. Puglisi."

"Best researcher in the business," Peewee said, and gave Nino a pat on the back.

Peewee grabbed three glasses of wine, handing one to Phil and one to Nino before claiming the third for himself. Then glanced over at Anne. He quickly looked away, apparently reluctant to engage in a conversation with her. He pushed his glasses up to the bridge of his nose.

Phil asked Peewee about his writing process. "Where do you get your inspiration?"

Peewee talked about research, and how there was no end to the inspiration he could get from news articles. But also how he'd had the opportunity to talk to people who'd worked in the mafia. That made me think of Primo Leone, owner of Carmine's only taxi company. Primo was a former driver for the mob. I wondered if Peewee had ever talked to him.

Peewee put an arm around Nino's shoulder. "If it wasn't for Nino's research, I wouldn't be able to write the books. At least not as fast as I do now. My readers are always chomping at the bit for a new installment in the Frankie F. saga. I swear, if I jotted down a bit of Frankie's dialogue on a napkin, it would sell at auction."

He laughed, a donkey's guffaw.

Anne teetered on her heels and nearly fell. She raised her briefcase, brandishing it. "I've got a big ol' napkin right in here..."

Nino caught her before she toppled over. "Come on, Anne. I think you need to lie down."

"There's a couch in the office," Phil said, a worried look on his face.

With a hand around Anne's back, Nino led her toward the office in the back. She seemed half-unconscious, but as I watched them walk away, something strange happened.

The moment before Nino pulled her through the door to the office, Anne slipped a hand into one of his jacket pockets—very much as if she were pickpocketing him.

Now, why would she do that?

"ABSOLUTELY DEAD," Phil said, and sank onto a chair by the food station. "Dead on my feet."

He took off one of his brogues and massaged his foot.

There was lots of commotion as people found their coats, finished drinks, and went in and out of the restroom —one thriller author drunkenly wandering into the dark back office before realizing his mistake—but now Milano Books was finally quieting down. The last of the guests had left. Phil had locked the door behind them. The only people remaining were the "crew members," plus the Rizzolis.

Angelica and I were cleaning up the food station, which had turned into a mess of empty glasses and bottles, discarded paper plates, and half-filled cups with water and other beverages. There were also books, picked off shelves for consideration or conversation, and then discarded next to a wine glass.

One of the books was Giuseppe Di Lampedusa's *The Leopard*. Another was Agatha Christie's *Evil Under the Sun*, which I'd read several times. I stacked them on a third book, one of Peewee's called *The Killer's Cabin*, and returned them to their shelves.

Phil said, "I haven't been so nervous since I went on tour with Tarantella."

Before becoming a bookstore owner, Phil had briefly enjoyed one-hit-wonder fame with a hard rock band, in which the big hair was as memorable as the music. It was difficult to imagine that, decades ago, this bald, cardigan-wearing bookseller had once worn purple tights. But then I bet people who knew about my past wondered at the trans-formation I'd undergone, from TV detective Eve Silver to small-town Bernie Smyth.

"The event was a success," Peewee said, coming back from the restroom. "Don't you think so, Nino?"

Nino nodded.

"You really think so?" Phil said. "Well, I hope it won't be the last time you come to read at Milano Books."

"I'm sure it isn't," Peewee said, smiling his big-toothed smiled and then covering his mouth as he stifled a yawn.

Across the room, Nat and Mrs. Viola were packing up the historical society's artifacts.

"Where's the hatchet?" Mrs. Viola asked.

"I packed it already."

Nat was putting the Tommy gun in a bag on the table.

"Not like that—you'll scratch it," Mrs. Viola said, and she grabbed the gun and a different bag and began to pack it herself, wrapping it in bubble wrap. "And it goes in this other bag. I didn't track down all these objects, identify them, catalog them, only to have you lose them…"

Nat watched her, hands on his hips, and a rueful twist to his mouth. I'd never watched him work with Mrs. Viola, and I was amazed he could tolerate her fussiness. But then he was the most even-keeled person I knew. Even as I watched, Nat gave a shrug and started stacking the historical photographs, checking each off an inventory list.

Angelica brought my attention back to the food station.

"All these glasses have to go out back. As do the empty bottles."

I placed the empty bottles in boxes and the glasses on trays, getting ready to carry them out back.

"I'll help you," Nat said, joining me at the table. He leaned close and whispered, "Mrs. Viola has banished me from her kingdom. She says she can't keep track of things if I keep putting them away, and now she's going back over the entire inventory to make sure we haven't missed anything. She's sure I misplaced something."

"Attention to detail," I said.

"That's one word for it."

I picked up a box of wine bottles. Nat grabbed a tray of glasses.

"Here, let me be helpful," Roberto said, picking up a tray as well.

Silently, Nino joined the expedition, picking up a box of wine bottles, and then another, stacking it on top of the first.

At the office door, Nino held his boxes with one strong arm and pushed open the door. It was pitch black inside, and yet I knew roughly where to put the box, so I crossed the room.

I got halfway. My feet caught something on the floor, like

a piece of furniture, firm and unmovable, and I tripped. The box hit the floor with a thud, followed by a loud clatter of empty bottles rolling out as I landed on my hands and knees in the dark.

"Hey, Bernie—you all right?" Nat called out, and then I heard a click—apparently the light switch—and the overhead fluorescent tubes flickered to life. Bright light dispelled the darkness, and I had to blink to adjust to it.

The first thing I saw was Anne's briefcase on the floor. A hairpin was jammed into the lock, and there were scratches all around, as if someone had tried, unsuccessfully, to open it.

Then I heard Nino curse and Roberto mutter half a prayer, and I turned to look back at what I'd stumbled over.

It was Anne. She lay still.

"Quick, we need to get help," I said, as I scrambled to my feet.

Nat was the first out the door, then I followed, and the two others behind me.

As Nat was announcing what had happened, I reached Phil and whispered, "Make sure all doors are locked and no one can get out."

His eyes widened with shock, but he nodded.

Then chaos erupted.

"Murder!" Mrs. Viola cried out, her voice rising to a hysterical pitch.

Peewee cursed, pushing people out of his way. "I need to see her—where is she?"

"I've got Chief Tedesco on the line," Angelica said.

"Where's my husband?" Gina wailed. "Where is Roberto?!"

"I'm right here."

"Thank God." She rushed at him and clung to him, arms wrapped tight. "I thought maybe…"

Phil checked the front door was locked. Then headed for the office, and I went with him.

He checked that the office back door was locked.

"It was open," Phil said. "But it's locked now."

He backed out of the office, exhibiting a perfectly normal squeamishness at seeing a corpse. I'd hate to say it, but I was beginning to get used to it.

Nat came into the room and joined me. The two of us stood over Anne's dead body.

She was lying on her side, her face contorted in death. Her neck bore the marks of scratching and, most shockingly, a deep groove across. She'd apparently been strangled—my guess was with some kind of rope or wire.

"Something's wrong."

"You don't say," Nat said. "While we were drinking wine and talking books, Anne Adams was being murdered back here."

"No, Nat. I mean, about her briefcase."

He grabbed my arm, shocked. "Hey, you're right."

We looked at each other.

"It's gone," I said.

Want more? Keep reading book 4:
Meatballs, Mafia, and Murder

MORE BY M.P. BLACK

A Wonderland Books Cozy Mystery Series

A Bookshop to Die For

A Theater to Die For

A Halloween to Die For

A Christmas to Die For

An Italian-American Cozy Mystery Series

The Soggy Cannoli Murder

Sambuca, Secrets, and Murder

Tastes Like Murder

Meatballs, Mafia, and Murder

Short stories

The Italian Cream Cake Murder

ABOUT THE AUTHOR

M.P. Black writes fun cozies with an emphasis on food, books, and travel—and, of course, a good old murder mystery.

In addition to writing and publishing his own books, he helps others fulfill their author dreams too.

M.P. Black has lived in many places, including Austria, Costa Rica, and the United Kingdom. Today, he lives in Copenhagen, Denmark, with his family.

Join M.P. Black's free newsletter for updates on books and special deals:

https://mpblackbooks.com/newsletter/